ALSO BY THE AUTHOR

THE PLATINUM BRIEFCASE

D1372541

TOO CLOSE
FOR COMFORT

sands press
Brockville, Ontario

TOO CLOSE FOR COMFORT

Henry Cline

sands press

sands press

A Division of 10361976 Canada Inc.
300 Central Avenue West
Brockville, Ontario
K6V 5V2

Toll Free 1-800-563-0911 or 613-345-2687
http://www.sandspress.com

ISBN 978-1-988281-39-1

Cover Design by Kristine Barker and Wendy Treverton
Edited by Katrina Geenevasen
Formatting by Renee Hare
Publisher Kristine Barker

Publisher's Note

For information on bulk purchases of this book or any book published by Sands Press, please call 1-800-563-0911.

1st Printing April 2018

To book an author for your live event, please call: 1-800-563-0911

Sands Press is a literary publisher interested in new and established authors wishing to develop and market their product. For more information please visit our website at www.sandspress.com.

Dedicated in memory of my late grandma, who at ninety-one years old, still enjoyed the heck out of this book. I hope you do as well.

PROLOGUE

Sam Miller is… Or, was, my best friend.

I'm sorry, it just seems hard to know how to word it once someone who was so close to you decides to take their own life. Do I say he'll always be my best friend, or since he committed suicide, would I say he was..?

And if I say he was, does that make it seem like I don't care? Because I do. I cared more than I thought anyone else did, up to a point where I ended up figuring everything out with almost no help at all.

I'm not trying to sound like a hero or anything of the sort. But I am trying to say that I, Jack Sampson, solved the case that most believed did not exist.

I speak very vaguely now, but soon, it'll all make sense.

Chapter One
The Funeral
Stanton, Michigan
Friday, May 18th
2 pm

I lived in a small town called Stanton. Not like the island in New York, but... Actually, never mind. It doesn't really matter why it's called what it is called.

It was a nice town though, where everyone knew each other for the most part, and it was hidden by a few miles of forest and greenery. Never had a day that was hotter than ninety degrees and never cooler than thirty. Most liked it that way, and that's why they moved here, but others lived here for the quiet community and the small town feel. Just one grocery store that wasn't a Wal-Mart, one church, one elementary school, one middle school, one high school, houses here and there but not everywhere, and a town square with a police station, a fire station, a minuscule urgent care center, and a few other shops that went down what we called the Stanton Stretch.

My name's Jack Sampson and I am a senior in high school. I turned eighteen just a few months ago, but I haven't really discovered what the big deal was about it. I didn't want to smoke, I didn't have the urge to buy a gun since my dad left some behind, and I didn't have enough money or angst to move out of my house just yet.

I love my Mom. She's caring, sweet, and sensitive, but not to a point where it was annoying. Most kids were mad that my Mom was so cool to things and open minded for the most part, and they wished they had my mom for a Mom. But, they never want to trade me lives. You see, at Stanton High, I'm popular, but not in the way that most people like to be. I'm popular for the fact that my Father was killed overseas during his third deployment about three years ago. That's how I was remembered: The kid who didn't have a dad anymore.

But that's enough about me. Let's get to the real story.

My best friend, Sam Miller, decided to end his own life on May 14th, 2012, two and a half weeks before senior year was over. He was home alone

2

that Monday night just four days ago. His parents had gone out on a date to reinforce the stability of their marriage, although I don't know how much it helped once they got back to see their only child with segments of his head mixed in with the rest of the room's decor, and a pistol from his Dad's collection of guns lying beside his lifeless body.

On that night just four days ago, I was sitting in my room listening to music and messing around online, not really sure what, or if anything, was going to happen. I had already eaten dinner, and I was just waiting for myself to get tired. I remember being pretty happy that night, not really dreading anything or mourning the thought of my dad, but now I can't really fathom what happiness feels like. Not after all this shit.

But when Sam killed himself, you'll never guess how I found out.

Sadly enough, I first saw it on Facebook. One of Sam's cousins that I met during an awards ceremony at the end of eighth grade (who I thought was hot) posted a status saying that her cousin Sam had killed himself just moments ago. From all the sick jokes I had heard in high school, I thought this one was about to take the cake, but just as I started to comment on the status and chew her out for such a sick joke, I saw another status appear, saying the same thing had happened. Afterward, it was like a rainfall of statuses saying that they'd "miss Sam" and "Sam was a great guy" and that "Sam shouldn't have done it". By the time I read all the rainfall statuses, the parents of Sam Miller called me, wallowing in sobs as they explained, or tried to explain what had happened. Sam Miller, eighteen years old, killed himself out of nowhere.

Sam Miller was the most popular, genuine, and nice guy I've ever known, and I was lucky to have him as a best friend. He never hurt anyone or put people down. He did play football as the quarterback, but luckily, he wasn't a douche like most football players are depicted. Instead, he was raised by two of the best parents I've ever met in my life, who taught him to be himself, and not just something to please everyone else. Be somebody, not some*thing*. But in the idea of him being himself and to not please everyone else by doing otherwise, everyone actually liked Sam for who he was. No one ever made him feel bad about himself or second guess himself, or make him feel like he did something wrong. Sam was the kind of guy who never made an error, except twice: Once when we lost the last football game of the season, and then when he killed himself.

After Sam's parents called me, I entered a state of shock, where my phone kept buzzing with other texts and calls from kids at school who were trying to act like they cared about me and felt bad that I lost my best friend. A few of them I know actually cared, but most of them... I wasn't so sure about. After my dad was killed, I had the exact same thing happen as the six o'clock news exploited our loss the very next day, only two or three of the thirty people who texted me about my Father's passing actually approached me at school asking me how I was and if I'd be okay. One of those two or three people was Sam.

It was sort of odd to people that Sam and I were best friends, or that we even became best friends. He was a jock with a big heart, and I was a nobody with smarts and a receding heart. I mostly wore black accompanied with the same black hoodie, while Sam wore vibrant colors and a different jacket every day if it was chilly outside. Sam and I walked side-by-side in the halls, making each other laugh and really caring about one another. I think the night we discovered how much we cared about each other was one night after we saw a movie the summer before tenth grade, some guy started picking on me for a haircut I just got that looked like hell. To my delight, Sam stepped in and told the guy from a few cities over to back off. That's when the guy decided to come back with a few friends and his girlfriend so she could watch as he tried to beat us up. Sam and I fought these suckers for about ten minutes straight, and when one of us would go down, we'd reach down to help each other back up. Finally, we tired them out and they retreated. Sam and I, bruised and a little bloodied, looked at each other and Sam quoted a stupid song in a silly way that still makes me laugh today.

He looked at me, blood dripping from his nose, and he said, " *'I can tell that we are gonna be friends'.*"

That was the most memorable time we had together in our entire friendship. There were other times that were fun, but that was the one we talked about the most, and when school started, we told everyone that story, and everyone started to accept me not just as the kid who lost his father, but the kid who fought with Sam Miller. And we all know that anytime you can tell a story of how you fought somebody and won, everyone will love you. In fact, because of that story, I got my first serious girlfriend out of it.

But, that's another story...

*****

I drove by myself to the funeral. It was at the church just west of the Stanton Stretch. A Catholic church, one that Sam attended with his family every Sunday, and sometimes he went to the youth group sessions on Wednesdays, but he once told me he preferred the regular ceremonies instead of the youth group sessions.

I never went to church, but we all knew where the church was. It was almost completely surrounded by trees just west of the Stanton Stretch about two miles. I drove into the gravel parking lot and watched as all of the mourners in their black clothes stood outside the church and conversed or headed inside just to get it over with. I didn't go to school today so I could go to the ceremony because he was my best friend, but I saw some people at the funeral who never talked to Sam, posing that they cared. It started to piss me off, but I decided to just let them be.

I pulled up to the first concrete slab that wasn't occupied and I parked my car. Honestly, I didn't really care if the bumper hit the concrete. It was an old 1999 black Chevy Impala. I'm not saying I wasn't grateful that my mom had bought it for me with no strings attached, I just wasn't in the mood for caring about things. Not today at least.

Right as I stepped out of the car, I saw someone from school walking up to me and I braced myself for any tears that might try to force themselves out of my eyes.

It was Ben Whey, the only Laotian at our school. A few people found his broken English to be annoying and his mannerisms bizarre, but I liked him. He was kind and giving to most, unless they made fun of him. He approached me in a suave black suit with an intoxicatingly blue dress shirt and a bold black tie. He stood out, already being the best-dressed attendee to the funeral. I was in a suit, but I had only paid a hundred for the entire thing. I knew Ben had spent more than that on his.

Just as soon as he walked up to me, his arms stretched out and he embraced me; his eyes dampened my shoulder but I didn't push him off. Out of the few people who were nice to Ben, Sam and I were *always* nice to him.

In the midst of holding one another, he sniffled a few times and finally let go to face me. His short black hair stuck to his head like a magnet and he wiped at his eyes with his suit jacket sleeve. My brown hair was a little messed up from the hug and the wind, but I didn't mess with it.

"Jesus Christ," was the first thing Ben managed to say. "Never thought I'd be here for this."

"I never wanted to be here for this," I replied coldly.

Ben stepped to my side and patted my shoulder. We made our way to the church and a few people glanced over at us as they chatted: Just a bunch of kids from school or adults who I vaguely knew.

"You drove yourself?" Ben asked.

"Yeah. I didn't have any trouble driving."

"You're tough man... I had my parents drive me."

"I would've asked my Mom, but she works, so I didn't want to be a bother."

"You're acting like you'd ask her to tie your shoes? This is different, Jack."

"It sure as hell is different," I answered in a harsh way. "A lot different."

Ben decided to stray away from the topic of transportation and decided to say who was here.

"Principal Leonard is here, which is a little surprising," Ben commented.

"He was at my Dad's funeral too."

"Oh," Ben said, feeling like he was ruining my life. "Also, a few police officers are here, even Billy's cousin Donovan. You know, the only detective in this town?"

"Yeah, I know him," I answered, and I searched around really quickly. "I also see Chief Ramzorin."

Chief Ramzorin, Donovan Young, the Millers, and Principal Leonard were all huddled and talking. Donovan Young was the only detective in Stanton being that it's such a small town. He wore a scratchy looking suit along with a bold blue tie. He was in his late thirties and his black hair was short and ready for summer.

Chief Ramzorin was an old coot. I was surprised he hadn't retired yet, let alone complain or gloat about retiring. He was in his mid-seventies, but you couldn't even tell by how he walked, talked, and presented himself. The only thing that made his age noticeable was his knowledge. His white hair stuck up straight all around and he nodded with pain in his eyes as Mrs. Miller spoke. He wore his decorative uniform with medals and such hanging from it. I couldn't hear what they were saying, but I knew it wasn't anything happy.

Principal Leonard's fair red hair was shiny and perfect. The wind didn't dare mess it up, and he wore thick-rimmed glasses as he listened to Mrs. Miller's words. He wore an ugly brown suit and a tangerine tie. He never had much of a fashion sense, but neither did I.

"What do you think they're talking about?" Ben asked.

"Probably not about who won the game a few nights ago," I said dryly.

"Hah, no, I'd say they're not."

As I looked around, I noticed I didn't see someone who I was pretty sure would attend. But, since Ben seemed to know who all was here, I asked him.

"Is Emily Harper here?"

"Yeah, she's inside. She just talked to the family earlier, and then all the adults jumped in so Emily walked inside."

Emily Harper, also a senior, was Sam's perfect match. She was a cheerleader, but just like Sam, she was nice and sweet, not like the usual stereotype. Sam and Emily were always happy together and dated for two years continuously up until today. I didn't see her right now, but I knew I would later.

Ben and I seemed to stay outside though. I didn't go in yet because I wasn't ready to, and Ben just wanted to help me out and make sure I didn't collapse. He was almost too nice, and a part of me felt bad for thinking that I might not do the same for him if he was in my shoes.

Out of the crowd, I saw someone approaching me and Ben that I hadn't talked to in a while. An old best friend.

Billy Young appeared from the crowd and walked toward me in a navy blue suit, and the only way I made the distinction of the color was from the sun shining down right on him. He didn't look too happy as his tan face stared down when he walked up to us.

He and I related on the same level… almost. My Dad was killed and his parents were druggies. His cousin, Donovan (the detective in his thirties) adopted Billy and now they live together. Nobody knows what happened to Billy's parents now, but no one dares to ask Billy either.

Billy was almost as popular as Sam, but according to the girls, he was better looking. He worked out the summer before senior year and got all toned up and now girls drooled over him, but he acted like he couldn't tell. Before that, he only had leg strength from playing soccer, so we all knew he toned the rest of himself up for an extra bonus. A few years ago he used to hang out with me and Sam, but then he went his own way and started hanging out with all of the soccer team. Everyone goes their own way eventually, I guess.

Billy's short brown hair waved in the wind and he reached for it a few times to fix it. He wasn't happy, but then again, why would anyone be happy today?

"Hey, guys," Billy said calmly.

"Hi, Billy," I replied.

He sighed heavily and said, "This is so messed up."

"I know," Ben said. "Why would Sam do this?"

"Maybe he knew something the rest of us didn't, about life, or the afterlife, or something... Hell, I don't even know what I'm saying anymore," Billy rambled.

"If Sam really did have something he needed to say or something happened to him, he would've told me," I said, trying not to sound too haughty.

"I know, sorry," Billy said. "Sam was a good guy, we all know that. Something just got the best of him."

Sam wasn't that kind of person though, and that's what bugged me. The Sam Miller I knew never would have killed himself or even thought about it for a second. It was irrational and didn't make sense. Billy's words just rubbed me the wrong way, but I guess he was just as grim as I was about the whole thing.

"Have you talked to Emily?" I asked.

"Yeah, briefly. She's crying more than I've seen the parents cry," Billy said accusingly.

"I can't blame her," Ben said. "Relationships always end in high school, but not like this."

"I don't think their relationship would've ever ended," I commented. "They were perfect for each other."

Billy made a face and I made nothing of it. He knew it was true.

Donovan suddenly walked up behind Billy and said, "Hey, I think we should go ahead and be seated."

Billy nodded and looked back at us.

"See you later. Some of the kids from school are meeting up at Shakey's after the funeral. You both are welcome."

"Thanks, Billy, maybe I'll see you there," I replied.

With that, Billy strolled off with Donovan to the church and I faced Ben once again. Both of our eyes were filled with sorrow, and I only wondered for a second who could be in more pain over Sam's death. But, a question kept bugging me the entire time I was driving over to the church, and now standing before Ben, I just had to vocalize it.

"Why would Sam do this?" I asked, not necessarily expecting a real answer. "We're just a week and a half from graduating and getting out of the main hell hole… Why kill himself?"

Because of Sam's suicide, all of the happiness and awesomeness of graduation seemed to go away and never wanted to come back. Now, it was just a matter of how to survive without Sam.

Ben interrupted my thoughts with a simple, "I don't know. I really just don't know. It doesn't make any sense."

A week and a half: Eight actual days of school. What happened, Sam..?

Taking a moment to look away from Ben, I saw Principal Leonard along with Chief Ramzorin walking up to us as the Millers walked inside the church. Not everyone was going inside just yet; the bell would tell us when to congregate.

Ben turned his head to me slowly and asked, "Why do you think they're coming over here?"

Thinking Ben had something to hide, I answered, "They're probably just checking us out since the Millers probably said we were friends of Sam's."

"We always will be his friends," Ben corrected optimistically.

Principal Leonard was the first one to speak. His eyes didn't want to make contact with mine or Ben's, but they were forced to under the circumstances.

"Mr. Sampson," he addressed me, almost like I was an adult. Well, I was eighteen.

With a little hesitation, he stuck his hand out and presented it to me for a handshake. I didn't pull any gimmicks: I just gripped, shook, and released.

Chief Ramzorin didn't say anything to me, but instead, he looked at Ben and said, "Mr. Whey… is that right? Did I say it correctly?"

"Yes, just like if you were saying something 'weighs' this much," Ben explained, just like he did back in fourth grade when he moved here. That brought back some innocent memories.

"I hope this doesn't offend you, but we'd like to talk to Jack alone," Chief Ramzorin followed up.

"Oh no, that's fine," Ben said sincerely. "I'll go ahead and be seated. Jack, if you need anything, just find me, all right?"

"I know," I replied.

Ben walked off the best he could without stirring up the dirt onto his suit and I scoffed lightly. Once Principal Leonard spoke, I turned away from Ben and listened closely.

"Mr. Sampson," Principal Leonard spoke.

"Please, you don't have to be so polite. You called me Jack when I was beating up Raymond Todd, and you can call me that now."

"Hah," Principal Leonard laughed. "Yes, I remember that now. Wasn't your fault though, right?"

"That's what they all say," Chief Ramzorin said with a small smile, trying to lighten the mood. It didn't work for me.

"Look, Jack," Principal Leonard spoke in a hardened tone. "The Millers said you were really good friends with Sam, and I just wanted to extend my condolences to you as well. If you ever need anything at school, maybe some time away from class if it's too much for you, just come see me anytime."

"Well, thank you, Principal Leonard," I said, and then I looked at Chief Ramzorin. "So, why are you here?"

"Being the police chief of this town, I usually go to the funerals to show my concern," Chief Ramzorin said, defending his right to be here. "Also, I knew Sam. Well, not as good as you, and I won't act like I talked to him a lot either, but he helped the police food drive a few years back, and he was a good kid. I was also there at the games and lemme tell ya, I always supported what he did at the last game this year. It would've worked out if it wasn't for those steroids kids from Lincoln."

I shot him a look of surprise and asked, "You really think they were juiced?"

"Kid, the only time I've ever seen people that muscular also able to run fast was in some stupid Arnold Schwarzenegger movie," Chief Ramzorin said without a doubt in his mind.

I cracked a small smile, wondering how a police officer could be that cool. He sent one back to me, along with some comforting words.

"If you ever need something from me," he added, pulling out a little card from his breast pocket, "just give me a call."

"Thanks, Chief," I said as I took the card. I glanced at it before I put it in my pocket and it was just some standard information: Phone number, cell phone, email, and even a fax. Afterward, I slipped the card into my breast pocket and Chief Ramzorin patted my shoulder.

"Also," Principal Leonard said, "the Millers want you to sit by them if you don't mind, and I think they mentioned having you say a few words about Sam."

"I was about to ask them if I could. Thanks for the message."

Principal Leonard nodded while the Chief looked off at the church and saw that more people were moving inside. The Chief then turned back to me and said, "Well Jack, it looks like everything's about to start, so I'll be leaving you now. But, just remember, if something comes up, call me. Stay strong."

He patted my shoulder once more as I nodded to him and Principal Leonard. They walked off toward the opening of the large wooden doors. The white exterior stood out against the green and the gravel, and as I looked up, I saw a small tower extending from the rooftop with a cross in the circular window just below the peak. Something about it just seemed majestic and I tried to remember the last time I went to church. Maybe it was the last time my Dad's parents came into town.

Once I realized that I didn't really care much, the bell tolled and everyone started to cram into the church like hungry cows: Knew where they were going, but took a hell of a long time to get there. I trailed behind in the big crowd, seeing a few people I knew. Mister Grigsby, the owner of a small home improvement shop on the Stanton Stretch waddled in, along with his wife and some kid I'd never seen before. Mr. Saitov, the owner of the bowling alley on the Stanton Stretch, seemed to shuffle in very reluctantly. Mrs. Traven and a few members of her family were also attending. They owned the only bakery in town.

Then, I saw Raymond Todd, who I now had a good friendship with. The fight was all the way back in ninth grade, and now we just joked about it.

But then, I saw one person who I wasn't too crazy about seeing.

Alyssa Jackson, my old girlfriend, and the only one that I'd been serious with.

She looked at me, with her soft brown hair covering half of her left eye. Her black dress stretched down all the way to cover her ankles, and her flat bottom shoes gleamed a black glow that almost haunted me. Her lips moved just a touch to where I knew she was mouthing a "Hello" and her hand went up beside her face. I returned the hand gesture quickly and then looked forward.

We had broken up at the end of junior year... And please don't ask why. Just as Ben said earlier, all relationships in high school came to an end, unless you were really just that lucky. Some argument had turned vastly wrong, and lo and behold, we're not together anymore. Of course, now we were okay, but people still questioned both of us about why we weren't together anymore. It was probably the only question that upset me, besides anything about my dad.

Finally being able to enter, I spotted the Millers up ahead and the Father walked away from them in a bitter sorrow. I walked down the altar and I felt everyone's eyes burning into the back of my head. It seemed as though I was the last one getting seated, but I don't think they really blamed me. Way at the back just as I had entered, I saw all of the seniors from school mostly sitting together. Besides prom, this was the only other superficial thing that brought us closer together.

As I stepped beside the pew that the Millers filled, Mr. and Mrs. Miller darted their eyes to me and I could tell that some warmth was finally constructed from their hearts, which also showed in their eyes. Mr. Miller stayed strong in a tasteful suit but with a quiver in his lip every once in a while, I knew his eyes were about to start flowing like Niagara Falls.

Mrs. Miller tried wiping her nose under her black veil and her eyes darkened with every second that passed. But, just as I started walking by the people awkwardly, trying not to hit their knees, I saw that Mrs. Miller wasn't the last one in the pew, but rather, Emily Harper was sitting on her left. Emily motioned for me to come sit by her, but not in an exciting way like some friends would do at the movies, more of a cry for help.

The organ played a melodramatic tune and I felt my eyes burn. *Why must they make these so damn sad...?*

Just as I stepped in front of Mr. Miller, he stopped me gently and motioned me in. I leaned over, and his words were delicate.

"Did Principal Leonard or Chief Ramzorin speak to you about saying a few words about Sam?"

I nodded, and then added, "Yes, I'd love to."

"Great, that's fantastic," Mr. Miller said, and just for a moment, there was happiness in his eyes. "The Father will ask you to go up there when it's your time. Don't worry."

I nodded to show him I understood and he patted me on the back so I kept walking. Next, Mrs. Miller gave me a bittersweet smile and I returned one back. She wore a black veil but I could see how her face was. The only thing makeup couldn't cover was hurt.

Then, at the end of the pew with a spot saved for me, Emily gestured to the gap between her and Mrs. Miller and I filled it. Emily looked at me and we exchanged a few quick words.

"It's good that you're here. I didn't want to be stuck with just a bunch of adults," Emily started.

"Why wouldn't I come?" I asked, getting a little aggravated too easily.

"No, I knew you'd come. I just meant…"

"Oh, sorry," I said, realizing what she meant. "Just hard, you know?"

"Yes, I do."

And to my surprise, Emily reached over to my hand and grabbed it. We interlocked fingers and I felt out of place. Hopefully, Sam wasn't looking down on me in an angry way.

To start everything, the Father lifted his arms and the organ ceased playing. Once the room was quiet and the wooden doors at the back closed, I could already hear a large amount of sniffling and crying and coughing. It was like someone had locked us in and set off tear gas, but I think we all would've preferred that.

"Everyone," the Father started to ensure that people would quiet down. "Today, we gather to mourn the unexpected death of one of God's children. Sam Lee Miller died on May 14th, 2012, and he is now up in Heaven with God and all of the other ones we have lost in our lives…"

He continued on, talking about Sam like they were close buddies, but I knew that wasn't true. Sam didn't hang out with Fathers in his spare time. He talked to me or he hung out with Emily. The Father's way of talking about Sam upset me, but I let him continue. There was no way I was going to make a spectacle at Sam's funeral.

Eventually, the Father stopped talking and he looked out into the crowd directly at me.

"Jack, I believe you have something you want to say."

With slight hesitation, I started to stand up and Mrs. Miller patted my back just like all the other adults, and Emily released my hand so I could depart. Stepping out onto the side I didn't use earlier as everyone's eyes were on me, I headed for the front of the church to the podium where the Father had stood just seconds ago. Now, he stood off to the side and welcomed me to take his position and address the mourners. Part of me didn't want to do this anymore. My feet felt like they weighed a ton and the walk to the podium seemed to last a lifetime. Sam's lifetime...

And like Sam's life, there was an abrupt end to the walk and I found myself standing behind the podium, looking out upon everyone else. Their eyes fed on my presence and they waited for me to say something clever to lighten everything up, but I wasn't in the mood to lighten everything up.

Instead, I cleared my throat and started.

"Hi, I'm Jack Sampson; some of you know me as Sam's best friend, but others might not know me at all. But even though we might not all know each other, we're all here for the same reason: To honor Sam Miller and remember him as the great person that he was."

Suddenly, I felt the need to stop talking. Looking out at the crowd, I saw Ben Whey looking back at me, hoping I'd continue. Next, there was Billy Young along with Donovan, and they sat next to Chief Ramzorin and Principal Leonard. Billy wiped a tear away and I looked to the left at Alyssa, and some inappropriate thoughts ran through my mind because I was desperate to think of something else. At the back, Raymond Todd and his girlfriend Jennifer Rogers shared a quick sappy kiss full of tears and anxiety. Finally, looking back at Emily Harper and the Millers, in front of all my classmates, the elders and kids of the town, and God, I finished my speech by crying until I was led off by the Father and Emily.

CHAPTER TWO
SCHOOL
STANTON HIGH SCHOOL
MONDAY, MAY 21ST
7:57 AM

I hope it's not too obvious to say that I didn't feel like going to Shakey's after the funeral.

To make a metaphor, since my English teacher always asks me to, I'd say that I was feeling pretty "Shakey" once everything was said and done.

At the funeral, I just kept crying and crying and crying, even once I sat back down with Emily and Mrs. Miller. All I could do was listen to the rest of the ceremony. My tear ducts didn't care that it was my best friend's funeral, or maybe they did and that's why they released every tear that I hadn't shed since my Father's funeral.

All of the kids from school approached me after the funeral to make sure I was okay. Surprisingly, I took all of their concerns for my well-being sincerely, although I might've done that just because I was so vulnerable. Alyssa tried to talk to me after, but Emily and the Millers were too busy trying to get me to stop crying. Once I was in my car and I saw my pathetic reflection in the rearview mirror, I calmed down and forced myself to stop crying like some child that got his Legos taken away. But, no one blamed me for bawling my eyes out. Even Emily joined me once she grabbed me and led me back to our seat, where she continued to awkwardly hold my hand and rely on me for support. Honestly, I didn't mind, and after crying for a bit, I convinced myself that Sam would've wanted that.

I didn't go to Shakey's after the funeral; I didn't tell my mom about what happened at the funeral; I didn't answer any texts or calls the entire weekend after. I guess you could say I entered a deep state of depression that most of the emo kids at school only dreamed about and what I had nightmares about. I stayed in my room, reminiscing, and even looking over Sam's Facebook wall just to see if anyone else cared enough.

There were lots of kind words, but the thing that stood out to me was posted pretty late on Saturday night, when some jackass lowlife piece of shit posted on his wall asking if he could take Emily now that Sam was gone. I commented on it, spewing every cuss word and derogatory term that I knew at him and the post was removed by Mrs. Miller, who then questioned my sensibility. I apologized to her for the language, but not to the guy who posted that. He better be glad he's out of state.

But would I even really go after him, or is it just a state of mind that makes me feel better, to think that I actually would if I could? I didn't know.

After the spewing, I went back to my bed and cried for the rest of the night until I fell asleep. Feeling pretty pathetic on Sunday, I just sat around in my room, thinking that Sam would walk into my room and tell me it was just a sick joke like I thought before. Nothing bad ever happened in this town till now, which made this whole situation too close for comfort.

To try and relieve some of my pain, I thought back to ninth grade, and I remembered some other senior had killed himself the night of prom. But, he had a suicide note, explaining that he couldn't come out of the closet because of his militaristic dad and Catholic mom, and he felt it was the only thing left to do. Sam didn't have a suicide note or anything. That's what made it harder than anything else.

I thought about suicide a few times before, but not in a serious way. Just in a silly way, where I thought to myself, *Huh, what would I use to kill myself?*

Because of some terrible horror movie I saw a few years back, I thought of putting my hand down the sink and the garbage disposal would come on, and instead of just taking off my hand, my whole body would somehow fit down the sinkhole and get cut up in the garbage disposal, which made me think that the whole idea was just ridiculous and I'd end up laughing rather than actually doing it.

Why couldn't Sam have just laughed it off? Didn't he ever hear that it was the best medicine?

Or was that it? He was terminally ill and he just didn't want to tell anyone?

He once told me that he took himself to the doctor after getting his license the summer before tenth grade, and he still got a superhero sticker for any "boo-boo's" they left on him. I asked if he was getting tested for STD's and that's why he wanted to go alone. He laughed, shook his head, and replied, "Maybe if I did your dog."

"I don't have a dog?" I replied.

"Oh sorry, that's your Mother, I always forget."

Now thinking back on it… That was the only time Sam had ever really dissed me… and it was just a lame "Your mom" joke.

Why, Sam? Why'd you do it?

Not the joke, but the suicide… It was a rhetorical question, but I kept asking it to myself. Who wouldn't in this situation?

And even though I had a terrible weekend (although, it's not like a week of everyone talking about the suicide was a breeze), I decided to come to school today, on this "spectacular" Monday, and see all the great students and staff of Stanton High, and maybe, someone could make me laugh. Gary Vázquez usually had a joke. He was a Texas-born hombre who just happened to move north after his birth. Sometimes, he joked about popping out right after his parents jumped the border. He said the force that his mom felt from hitting the ground after jumping the fence made him pop out. He got detention last year for keeping the joke alive though, and now he didn't joke about it anymore.

As I pulled into the parking lot behind Stanton High, I saw a few sophomores leaning against some spoiled kid's Camaro who wanted to fight me earlier in the year because I "took his parking spot", even though the spots weren't assigned. But, just to get back at him, I threatened to key his car if he kept threatening me. That made him shut up.

When I pulled into the parking spot, the spoiled kid, Joey Daniels, sneered at me as I put my car in park. I turned down the radio and heard him talking, probably some shit on me before I stepped out. I tried not to care, but now, after the suicide, everything got under my skin pretty easily.

Pulling the keys out of the ignition to stop the incessant beeping of the car telling me I left them in, I slammed my car door and headed for the school without my backpack. They told us that these last few days of school, we just needed a pencil.

"Hey, Jack!"

I knew it was Joey's voice just by how he called me out. I turned to him, clenching my right hand into a fist and waiting for him to set me off.

I didn't even have to respond vocally for him to keep talking.

"You're a senior this year, right?" he asked, and all of his other stupid friends stared at me.

"That's right," I said.

"So I'll be able to take that spot next year, right?" he asked.

Surprised at what he was asking, I went along with it, hoping for the best.

"That's also right," I said.

He nodded, thinking he was pretty cool for talking to me in such a demeaning way. Luckily, I hadn't thought about ripping his head off just yet.

And when he seemed to be done asking me questions, I started to walk off and head to the school, but then, he called my attention back to him.

"Hey, Jack, also…"

His voice sort of trailed off toward the end of the sentence as I turned back toward him. His friends even looked at him, not expecting him to keep talking to me. But the expression on their faces made me think that Joey was about to make fun of me.

To my surprise, he didn't.

"I heard about Sam," Joey said, talking in a better tone now. "I just wanted to say I'm sorry."

I stared at him, just to make sure his statement was genuine, and eventually, I figured it was. But instead of complimenting him and saying that it was "big of him to say that" and I "really appreciated it" and "blah, blah, blah", I simply replied, "Thanks, Joey."

Once that was over with, I continued walking to the school, hoping that more people would be like Joey was about the whole situation. I mean, we're all mature, right?

"Jack, is that you?"

Douglas Floyd was heading my way from behind me and I didn't stop to look. By now in the school year, I could recognize all of the people in my grade just by hearing their voices. But I shouldn't brag too much, since there are only about eighty-five kids graduating in my senior class.

Douglas was a nice guy, standing tall at about six foot- three inches. He was hassled every damn day of each school year for not playing basketball, but he just felt that academics were more important. His blonde hair was always cut short, never even getting close to covering his eyebrows. He sort of slouched as he jogged up to me and started conversing. I felt short at five foot- eleven inches.

"Hey, Doug," I replied casually.

"Hey man, I texted you a bunch this weekend, but you never answered. I could understand that you didn't want to come to Shakey's, but we were all worried about you."

"Oh yeah?" I said as we headed to the school. "Who's 'we'?"

"All of us, man. You know... Everyone who went to Shakey's, which was basically everyone who's in our class. The only people who didn't go to Shakey's were you, and Emily."

"Well, I'm sure you didn't miss me and her too much. We just cried all weekend, to be honest."

"Gosh man, that's why I was texting you. I thought maybe I could cheer you up," Doug offered with the child-like cursing he was known for.

"Well, you talking to me now is getting the ball rolling," I answered.

"That's good... Speaking of people talking... Alyssa let her shake melt before she stopped talking at Shakey's... She kept talking about you."

"Really?" I said. "What was she saying about me?"

"Just... How she wishes she could've uh, helped you, or made you feel better. Nothing too personal or anything, just, how we all wanted to help you, man."

"Yeah, well, that's all right. I appreciate the concern."

"I hope you do, man," Doug said. "Everyone was worried that you might've... Well, we all just thought the worst, since you've already lost loved ones."

"I get it," I said hastily. "You're hinting at my Dad."

Doug shrugged and looked innocent.

"Well, I didn't wanna say it too strongly... I've never lost anyone close to me. Sam wasn't very close to me, but he's the closest anyone's ever come."

"It's not fun," I said simply.

"Oh no, I wouldn't call it that at all... Although I'm ignorant to the idea of losing a loved one, I still wouldn't call it fun."

"That's good Doug, you're learning something."

"I am?"

"Yeah," I replied. "You're learning that not everything is just peachy all the damn time, and that we all have to lose something eventually."

The way I spat that statement out made Doug shudder and I felt that he was afraid of me. I stopped for a second on the sidewalk, trying to collect myself before I started crying like I did over the weekend.

"You sure you want to come to school today?" Doug asked.

"Yeah, I'm sure... Only eight days, right?" I asked.

Doug shot me back an awkward smile and said, "Yeah, just eight days..."

I exhaled the toxins from my lungs and inhaled some fresh air to keep myself going. Doug led the way this time and we made our way to the commons area of the school where everyone would unfortunately be.

And right when we walked in, I felt everyone stop what they were doing and stare at me. For the first time ever, I noticed their eyes feasting upon me more than the stupid milk ads and anti-drug ads plastered all over the plain white walls.

Maybe Doug was right. Am I really in the mood for school today?

The other side of my head answered with a, *When am I in the mood for school?*

Maybe I would be if Sam was here.

I cringed, wanting all the thoughts and feelings for Sam to just go away, but everyone staring at me didn't make it easy.

Out of the crowd of eyes, Ben stood up and started walking toward me to relieve Doug of "Make sure Jack is okay" duty. Doug gave me a super delicate punch on the arm as he walked off and let Ben take care of me.

"Hey, buddy," Ben said.

"Hi," I said, biting my upper lip.

He noticed that I was looking back at everyone else who just had this un-please-able want to stare at me.

"If you don't look at them, they won't look at you anymore," Ben suggested.

I looked away for Ben's sake, but said, "That's what we'd all like to think."

Ben started walking with me to our first hour and he said, "We were all worried about you, Jack. I ended up calling your house to ask your mom how you were."

"What'd she say?"

"She said you were just locked up in your room, but that's what you wanted."

I nodded.

"Why's everyone so worried about me, Ben?"

"Because... Sam was your best friend, and you've already lost someone close before. At Shakey's... You were all we talked about... well, just you and Emily."

"I heard that Alyssa kept talking about me," I inquired.

"Yeah, she really did," Ben concurred as we curved down the hall.

A few teachers were standing outside their rooms talking about things that I didn't care about. They didn't have to deal with the loss of Sam, but we did.

Making sure I didn't stare any of the teachers down, I kept talking to Ben.

"What was Alyssa saying about me?" I asked, trying not to sound too concerned about it.

"We didn't go to Shakey's for gossip time," Ben started. "She just mentioned how you are a good person, and you loved Sam like a brother."

I was surprised Alyssa actually remembered me saying that. Sam was the brother I never had and the one I'd always wanted. In some ways, after my father was killed, I started taking advice from Sam instead, knowing that his personality was one to take advice from.

"Also, they were just staring at you in the commons because no one thought you were coming to school today," Ben added.

"Yeah? Well, I came to school after my Dad's death, so why's this any different? I don't want to wallow away in sadness any more than I have to."

"That's good," Ben said. "Sometimes you just have to go back to your normal routine to help adjust to something tragic."

"No, that's not it at all," I argued. "I just wanted to get out of bed and come to school."

The first bell rang to signify the beginning of another crappy school day. Ben still had some worries about my safety, but he decided to back off and end our conversation with a simple, "Okay, Jack. Here's our class, let's make the best of today."

"Shall we?" I asked, not expecting an answer.

Once we sat down in our seats and everyone flooded in, first hour began. I remember that Travis Porter came in a few minutes late, and Mrs. Reedman, the English IV teacher, joked that he'd have detention on one of the last days of school. He talked his way out of it, like most popular jocks do. The only way I'd get away with that was out of pity.

*****

Second hour: Calculus I. It was a class I wasn't too crazy about, but it helped the time go by. Mr. Harrison droned on and on about different things we'll see in college. Our exams were already finished, and now, it was just a matter of the future. Some other schools criticized how we did things, but I didn't mind too much. And, I wasn't even sure I wanted to go to college. Sam was saying that he'd get a football scholarship somewhere, and because of my smarts, I'd just follow him to the same college and we'd share a dorm together. Now that was hopeless. I now had to find my own college and go there on my own. Money wasn't an issue, but society was.

*****

Third hour: the worst hour of the day, usually was and today, it definitely was: Sociology. Gregory Allen, a suave asshole, decided to bring up Sam's suicide, and ask if there was anything in particular about it that made it stand out. Mr. Tinley talked about it for a while, but when he saw the permanent grave look on my face, he and the rest of the class looked at me and stopped talking about it. They didn't question me and ask what I thought about it. Maybe some other time, eh?

*****

Fourth hour we actually had some busy work in Government, but I wasn't too bothered by it since I had Emily there beside me. It was a partner activity, and immediately, Emily ran over to me and started to help. We didn't talk about Sam. It seems like we didn't have to. To us, it was just understood that this was a sad time and we needed each other. Surprisingly, to everyone in the class, Emily and I, or the two depressed kids in the class, actually finished our assignment first. Afterward, we talked.

"You didn't go to Shakey's either?" I asked.

"Hell no," Emily said. Her blonde hair was so shiny and alive that I wondered why I still felt sad. "I didn't want a bunch of people staring at me, waiting for me to start crying. I heard they mostly talked about you though, and this weekend, everyone texted me, wondering if I had talked to you. I said no, and that you probably just wanted to be left alone like me, and then I turned my phone off all day Sunday. It was, peaceful, to say the least."

"What about Alyssa?" I asked Emily, since they were pretty close friends. When I started to be really close friends with Sam, he was already dating Emily for a while, and Alyssa was right there, wanting a boyfriend. Somehow, it was almost perfect that Alyssa and I met that night at the bowling alley. It was just a little get-together, but it ended up being more than that.

"You'll like this girl, Jack. Trust me."

Sam's words echoed in my mind and I started to feel the tears again, but Emily interrupted them.

"Oh, she called me, saying she was too afraid to call you herself," Emily said. "You know, if you don't mind me asking, whatever happened between you two?"

"I don't even know the answer to that, Emily," I honestly said. "We had an argument, it turned ugly, and we parted ways."

"It can't be that simple," Emily said, trying to get more out of me. The fact that she was trying sort of annoyed me. "You guys were really great together... Not just one of those couples that were cute together, but you had something more than that."

"Well, when you or I can find out what that 'something more' is, I'll get back with her."

Emily shook her head lightly and complained, "No Jack... Don't be so gloomy. Maybe you two should hang out again, or go do something. I know she's not the only one who wants to."

"Maybe some other day, but not tonight," I said. "I'm not in the mood."

"Neither am I," Emily said, trying to hold my hand once more.

This time, a few eavesdroppers turned their heads toward us and I lowered our hands behind our pulled together desks in hopes that they couldn't see our hands interlocked. I wasn't in the mood for some fun with Alyssa, but I definitely didn't want any drama with Emily.

*****

When the bell rang, Emily and I walked out of the class together to head on over to fifth hour, which was an hour that Emily, Alyssa, Doug, Sam, and I shared together: Humanities.

Walking in through the doorway, I saw that Doug was already sitting in his seat. He was always early, and I never understood why. This class was terrible, besides the fact that we got to sit by each other and make jokes. But today, the class would be even worse, now that Sam was gone.

At the classroom doorway, Alyssa ran into Emily and me and felt the need to have a conversation.

"Oh, hi, Emily, and Jack," she said softly. More random thoughts of Alyssa and me together again flew through my mind and I shifted awkwardly to have Emily closest to Alyssa.

"Hi," Emily returned.

"I'm glad you guys are here," Alyssa said.

"Where else would we be?" I asked, then noticing by Alyssa's reaction that I used the wrong tone of voice.

"Well... Home I guess?" Alyssa said. "Emily, could I talk to Jack?"

"Aren't you already?" Emily asked, jokingly.

"I meant alone..."

"I know you did," Emily said, giving me a small wink. "Don't talk too long, class is about to start."

Emily strolled off, making her way to her seat that was behind Doug. She started a conversation with him as I began my endeavor with Alyssa.

"So, Jack... I'm sorry about the funeral."

"What about it?" I asked, not sure what she meant.

"Well, I mean, I had a spot open for you beside me when the ceremony started, but you were asked to sit by the Millers, so I understand. Also, I tried finding you after the ceremony, but the group around you was so big that I couldn't get through."

"Oh," I said. "Well, that's okay. It's the thought that counts."

"I hope you actually think that," Alyssa said. "Because, I was thinking, maybe... well, we ended on a bad note, and I was wondering if maybe..."

"Alyssa," I stopped her abruptly. A hot flash went over me and I felt out of place. "I don't think this is the time or place to talk about this."

"Well maybe if you didn't ignore everyone this weekend, we could've talked about it then..."

"Look, I appreciate the offer and all, but I'm telling you in the nicest way possible that now is not the time. How about... in a few days, if you still feel the same, you can give me a call and we can figure something out, okay?"

"Okay..." Alyssa said. "But, you won't be ignoring everyone again, right?"

"Not you," I said, and I walked off to my desk that was behind Emily.

The late bell rang and Alyssa made her way to her seat which was to the right of Doug. Once I sat down, Emily gave me a look but I shook it off. I didn't get why she thought she was Hitch. I didn't want to date Alyssa right now, not with everything that's been going on. And besides, it wasn't that easy. Eventually, I knew Alyssa would bring up the argument and we'd argue about it again, trying to determine who was right and who was wrong, even though deep down, we were both wrong.

But to really bring my mood to a new low, when all of the students shuffled in, I saw the one thing that I didn't think about until that moment.

Sam's empty desk was the dark hole in the room.

Right when we started class, Miss Hannah saw the empty desk and stared at it for a few seconds before actually starting class. Eventually, everyone was staring at Sam's old desk to the right of Emily, wondering what had gone wrong. In that few seconds, I think all of the students in the room felt the same way about the situation and wondered the same thing that I had since day one.

Just the simple, Why?

*****

After fifth hour was second lunch, or basically, the lunch I went to. Only a few seniors occupied first lunch along with a ton of sophomores and even freshmen. They weren't any of the seniors I liked though, so I didn't really mind.

The underclassmen were multiplying. Although my class of 2012 was just a mere eighty-five strong, the juniors had a class of two hundred, followed by the sophomores in the three hundred range, and the freshmen? I didn't even want to count. And gladly, I didn't have to. I just sat by some fellow seniors at my lunch usually, or I sat with Sam.

Dammit... Sam, Sam, Sam, Sam, Sam. There, maybe now he won't be stuck in my head so much. That's all I can think about. "What if" and "Maybe" were the two things running through my head, followed by Sam's name or his face appearing in my head. With my dad, after a few weeks, I started to forget what he looked like, but the pictures around the house reminded me of who he was. Now, if Sam's image started to disappear from my memory, I could just look on Facebook or the yearbook, but that'd never be enough.

I walked to the lunch line that led into a small room. I was perturbed and easily upset. A few kids' eyes wandered over to me and made sure I wasn't about to flip out. Even the freshmen knew who Sam was, and they knew who I was in relation to Sam. They gave me troubled looks, almost like an invitation to start bawling on one of their shoulders, but I turned them down. While in line, some nice girl ahead of me offered for me to cut her and get my food.

"No, that wouldn't be fair," I replied.

"C'mon Jack, we don't mind," another kid in line said.

That's when they all started signaling for me to go up to where the girl was motioning me and I finally took it just so they'd shut up, but I also thanked them. Every other day of this year, people hadn't been so nice to me, especially the underclassmen. That's because I wasn't very approachable, and I didn't let myself be. I was a cactus: Alone, hard to get close to, and living off of almost nothing. But this time, someone reached out to me just so I could get my lunch quicker. I knew I definitely wasn't a sight for sore eyes, but instead, I made their eyes sore.

I stepped in front of the girl, whose name I don't recall, and I grabbed a turkey and cheese sandwich from the line. Even the lunch lady observed me as I walked on by. Nobody would ever look at me the same way, but when had everyone looked at me in a better way?

The question floated away from me pretty quickly, and I made my way through the line, paid for my lunch, and walked out into the commons area. This time, most everyone was feasting their eyes on their feasts instead of me, and a small feeling of relief came over me. Maybe I could eat my lunch in peace and quiet, both literally and figuratively.

The sound of everyone's conversations bounced around the walls and I felt more alone than ever as I walked around, trying to find a place to sit. Emily hadn't mentioned eating lunch with me, so I tried finding someone else to eat with.

Soon enough, I saw Harold Vero with his bifocals and striped plaid polo sitting by a few of his mildly geeky friends, but not to a point where they were annoying. I first met Harold back in sixth grade, when we formed little groups after elementary school to survive in the big times. Hah, thinking of middle school as the "big times"...

Anyway, he didn't look my way, but I knew I was always welcomed to their table. So, cashing in my rain check, I sat down beside Harold and tried to not make a big scene about it.

But, Harold did.

"Hey buddy!" he shouted, speaking in a way that no one else had toward me all day. "What's new?"

"Nothing good," I replied, unwrapping my sandwich from the tin foil.

Harold hesitated, so Mark Collins said something. He was cool too, but we never hung out outside of school. He was just one of those nice guys you could usually rely on in school.

"Did you get the new Grave Robber game on Steam?" Mark asked.

"You know I'm a console gamer, Mark, not a PC."

"Mark's not a PC gamer either," Nick Wallace said, spitting a little when he talked. None of his saliva got on me though, but I wasn't so sure about my sandwich. He was the nerdiest of the group with his black thick-rimmed glasses and his superior attitude. When he spit like that and adjusted his glasses, I knew he was about to tell a joke. "He has a Mac."

"Oh, yeah, sorry, hope I didn't offend you, Mark," I said half-heartedly. Mark shook his head.

"So," I said, even though I tried avoiding anything related to Sam. "Did you guys go to Shakey's after the funeral?"

"No, we actually went to Robin's Pizza and just shared a large pepperoni with extra cheese," Harold said, and the way he talked now, I knew that before, he was trying to cheer me up, but it didn't work.

Nice try, Harold.

"Oh, okay," I answered.

"Yeah, only way I would've gone to Shakey's is if Sam was there too," Harold added. "Otherwise, we'd get picked on till... Well, till we left I guess."

"Or," said Nick, spitting a little and adjusting his glasses, "until there was nothing left to pick, like a nose after allergy season."

"Nice picture," I commented.

"You didn't go to Shakey's either," Mark accused.

"Yeah, but that was my choice," I said.

"Why didn't you?" Nick said, adjusting his glasses yet again, but no spitting. "I heard Alyssa wants to have a playdate with you soon."

"Can you grow up?" I asked harshly. Nick backed off and I continued, "Nothing is going on between me and Alyssa and I doubt it will."

"That's a shame," Mark said.

"Yeah, a real shame, Jack," Harold agreed. "I would kill for a girl like Alyssa."

"Killing people on WoW doesn't count, Harold," I said with such strong sarcasm I almost choked on my sandwich.

"Yeah, I know that," Harold said, a little mad that I mentioned the game. "Emily didn't go to Shakey's either, but I don't blame her, and I didn't necessarily blame you either, Jack."

"Well, thanks," I said. "Everyone else thought I was going to go off myself too."

"You wouldn't do that though," Harold said, and Mark nodded with Nick.

"Yeah, but that's also what everyone thought about Sam," I seethed, and then I noticed that I had already eaten my sandwich. For as skinny as

I was, I sure ate quickly. But once I realized I didn't really want to talk with them anymore, I started to stand up and I said, "I need to go."

"Gotta go, gotta go," Nick sang softly.

"Bye Jack, sit by us anytime you want," Harold said.

I nodded as I walked off, and I felt a few eyes were on me. Looking around, I saw the restrooms on the other side of the commons and I decided to use them.

Two juniors were standing at the water fountain eying some girl at another table. I passed by them to enter the bathroom and they didn't look at me. They kept egging each other on to make a pass at the girl, but neither one had the confidence or self-esteem to do it. I would've tried, just to get a laugh, but as usual, I just wasn't in the mood.

After using the bathroom and washing my hands unlike most kids, I walked out and saw that both of the juniors had walked over to talk to the girl. One of them reminded me of Sam, and the other reminded me of me. But, everyone's different.

As I started walking out into the commons again not really sure where to go, out of the corner of my eye, I saw a familiar face stand up from the "Asian table" and I immediately knew who it was.

Ben Whey started coming my way.

Today, he was wearing something a little less flashy, but still in style. Out of all of the pretty boys in this school, Ben got the least recognition, mainly because he wasn't a jerk like the other pretty boys. I always thought that if he walked up to me, his clothes would wrinkle and be scared of my clothes, but they never did that. It was only personified in my mind.

But when Ben approached me, there was something different about his attitude and mannerisms. He looked shocked and worried, not supporting and nice like before. I knew before he even said anything that something was up, even when he stood up from his table, all of the people at his table watched as he walked up to me. Before I could even tempt fate and see if this day was going to get worse, I knew it would get worse anyway.

"Jack," Ben said directly. "I have something I want to talk to you about."

"Well, what is it?" I ordered. "Spit it out."

"No, I can't here, too many people. How about after school, I'll meet you by your car," Ben said, his eyes flying around the room.

"Jesus, Ben, looks like you're tripping balls or something," I said, even though that wasn't in my normal vocabulary.

Ben shook his head and replied, "No, you know I don't do that stuff. Just meet me at your car after school, okay?"

"Got it," I said, and we parted ways.

Now, not knowing where to go or what to think, I stood by the bathrooms in the commons area just wondering what Ben had to tell me.

I just hoped it wasn't too bad.

*****

Lunch ended so sixth hour could begin: Chemistry II. It was a class I was forced to sign up into. Last year, my Chemistry I teacher, Mrs. Turner, said that I should really pursue chemistry, maybe even in the professional world. As much as I didn't want to go onto Chemistry II, she kept pushing it to me. I didn't want to take it, mainly because I knew it'd be a bunch of juniors or brainiac sophomores who skipped Biology in ninth grade and went right to Chemistry. But I was good at it, and after the twenty-minute lectures given by Miss Klein, I'd finish my work in about ten minutes. Or if I was lucky, she'd hand out the paper during her lecture and I'd just do the work along with her. That was easy enough.

Today was a lesson on life, and I wondered if she knew Sam, because she kept talking about living life to the fullest and making every day count and most importantly, don't let the little things bug you. She spoke truth and wisdom, but I wasn't completely sure why. In fact, after class, I finally popped the question and asked if she knew Sam.

"Yes, I did. He actually took this class last year, and he mentioned that you were his best friend at the beginning of the year during the 'get-to-know-you' part," Miss Klein explained.

"Was he good at this class?" I asked.

"Best in the class, both with his work and attitude," she said, and a teardrop ran down her cheek.

*****

Ultimately, it was now seventh hour, or last hour: Journalism. If I had ever taken such a BS elective, it would be Journalism. I'm not saying it's a BS class everywhere, but the teacher definitely made it that way.

Mrs. Waverly: All she did, every single day, was make us read a story out of the newspaper, or a magazine, or anything published (besides books), and then write about what the reporter did right and what the reporter did wrong. After that, we could do whatever we wanted. One time, when she wasn't looking, some kid actually lit a cigarette and started smoking, and all she asked was if it was hot in the class.

Finishing my work, I saw Billy Young toward the front row just starting on his. Beforehand, he was talking to some petite black girl with almost no reputation at all. I could tell by the desperation in his eyes that he just wanted something to make him happy, but she didn't do it for him. Not completely, anyway. Then for some reason, I started to wonder if he had a girlfriend... I thought he did...

Oh well, not important. If he did, then he knew what he was doing was wrong.

*****

Finally, school ended and I headed out to my car along with all of the other kids. As opposed to this morning, a bunch of kids were now smiling and laughing about how school was about to end and how everything was going great for them. Some of them were people who I thought were pretty close to Sam, but I guess not.

I waited at my car for about five minutes, and the traffic in the parking lot seemed to die down; still, no sign of Ben. Maybe he was just messing with me about having to tell me something. Maybe there was nothing really to tell. I actually hoped that was the case.

But no, soon, he came running to me down the concrete sidewalk that led to the red and black Stanton High, his hands filled with papers and his face red as an apple. It was comical, but I wasn't in the mood to laugh.

He ran up next to me and I almost had to reach my hand out to stop him from running into me. He started panting and explained between breaths, "Sorry... It was... the last... NHS meeting... of the year... and I forgot about it... So I ran... because I didn't tell you about it... and I felt bad."

"Take it easy, Ben," I said with a small laugh. "Catch your breath and then tell me what you wanted to earlier."

So, he took a moment to breathe and sort the papers into a more organized stack. Once he did that, he started to explain what was happening.

"Okay, now Jack, this is going to sound really crazy when I say it, but just bear with me, okay?"

"Okay?" I said, not sure what to expect at all.

"It's about Sam," Ben said.

"Of course it is," I complained. "I try to get him out of my head all day but he's always the focal point of every conversation I get into."

"Wait, you might take it as good news," Ben reassured.

"Hah! Good news after what happened? I doubt it."

"Jack, listen to me," Ben pleaded. I knew it had to be serious now. Usually Ben was the silly one.

"Yeah, okay, I'm listening," I replied.

Ben hesitated but eventually decided to give it to me straight.

"Well, what if I told you that Sam was murdered?"

His words hit me like a rolling stone that turned into a boulder and smashed our little town flat. Trying to forgive myself for the poor analogy, I looked at Ben dumbfounded and asked, "Murdered!? Why the hell would you even say that? Sam committing suicide is one thing, but the thought of someone killing him? Why would anyone do that?"

"Look, Jack, think about it. No one thought that Sam would ever kill himself, so why do we have to believe that? I think it was murder. I've been thinking about it all last weekend and today, and I wanted to wait to tell you until now."

Someone killing Sam?

Why would anyone do such a thing? Suicide was one crazy thing to fathom, but now murder?

"Who would've killed Sam?" I asked.

"I don't know… a student?"

"Why?"

"Jealousy, maybe? I don't know Jack… But it just doesn't make sense that Sam would commit suicide. You and I both know that. Even the Millers know that. Everyone in Stanton knows that Sam wouldn't kill himself unless he had a damn good reason."

Everything he said made sense, for the most part. It was true. Even the Millers doubted the idea that their only child, Sam, would kill himself. It just… Nothing could ever make Sam think it was a good idea to do that. *What the hell is going on…?*

"Okay," I said, trying to collect my thoughts and sort the sane ones into the sane file and the insane ones with the insane file. "Even if Sam was murdered… Well, what the hell are we supposed to do about it?"

"Well," Ben started, and I knew this wasn't going to be pretty. "Maybe you could run the idea by the police?"

"Why do I have to?" I asked.

"Because! I'm already late getting home and they seemed to like you at the funeral. I mean, the Chief told me to buzz off so he could talk with you!"

"That's true…" I said, now wondering if that's what Chief Ramzorin meant when he gave me his card.

If something comes up, call me…

Maybe he wouldn't think I was crazy if I told him our idea.

"I don't know, Ben… Sounds like a stretch."

"Hey, if they know that the people are concerned, they'll probably look into it!" Ben assured.

I kept thinking the whole situation over. As much as I hated it already, making it now a murder just made it ten times worse.

"You really think it's a murder?" I asked to clarify.

"Yes! I'm not going to send the police on some wild goose chase! I'm serious about all of this," Ben said.

I sighed, not wanting to agree with him, but I had to. Sam's suicide was a mystery from the beginning, a mystery that everyone else seemed to ignore. People just thought that was the way things were. Sam killed himself, and that's it.

But not to me and Ben… we knew better than that.

"Okay Ben, I'll go to the police station right now and see if I can talk to Chief Ramzorin," I promised as I dug out my keys from my pocket.

"Great, keep in touch," Ben said as he showed me his cell phone.

"Yeah, I know," I said.

Getting into my car and slamming the door closed, I felt mad. What sick bastard at my school would want to kill Sam? That's like when the Grinch wanted to steal Christmas, except whoever killed Sam couldn't bring him back.

CHAPTER THREE
THE POLICE

I headed west for the Stanton Stretch. That was the only way I knew how to get to the police station. Basically, the city was set up in a very simplistic way. Far south was where most of the homes were and where I lived, aka, a neighborhood known as Stanton Place. As you headed north from there, you would start driving down the Stanton Stretch for about a mile and a half, unless after a mile, you wanted to turn east or west at the light. Turning west would result in a small split of road between the shops that led to the church where the funeral was held, and turning right would result in passing by a few fast food restaurants and eventually getting to the school, which was then surrounded by a few lower-class homes in a place we liked to call Forest Haven. Farther north up the Stanton Stretch, you'd reach the only grocery store in town called "Value Mart" on the left side, and the police station was to the right, which is where I was headed. And the whole town was engulfed in a nameless forest.

The Stanton Stretch actually had a lot of things to do. The movie theater was tiny, but just because it was a tiny town. It was like the old movie theaters, with the transparent plastic billboard accompanied by the bold black letters and an array of lights behind it to show off what movies were playing. Most of the kids at school got jobs there or at the fast food restaurants and none of them ever complained. Although, it was awkward if you went on a date with the ticket person's ex... Not like I have any experience with that.

Across from the movie theater on the west side was the bowling alley. A lot of people's first "events" took place there, and just next to it was Robin's Pizza, where a lot of people's *last* "events" took place. But, there were no grudges held against anyone, for the most part.

Besides McDonald's and Wendy's and Taco Bell and all the other average and obvious fast food places, one was Shakey's, which was where all of my "friends" went after the funeral and felt it was a sin that I didn't go. Sorry guys, I just didn't feel the need to listen to fifties music and suck on a shake that would make you pass out before it actually came through the straw, and my words are not a dramatization.

But, way up north even past the small shops on the Stanton Stretch and past the police station and Value Mart, there was a little casual dining restaurant called Victor's Diner where you could never go wrong with choosing a burger. They also had a bunch of other foods, like pizza and steak and salad and fish, but like I said, just get a burger. It was the place that most of the adults went to, or the high school dates who were finally unlatching the fat "lock" on their wallets so they could take the girl somewhere nice. My mom and I ate there about once every two weeks, but other than that, I either got myself fast food or my mom cooked.

Heading up the Stanton Stretch and making my way to the police station with no traffic whatsoever, I passed the movie theater and thought about that night with Sam; the night that he knew we were going to be friends. Hah... Still makes me laugh now, even in the darkness of everything. But maybe going to the police station would shed a much-needed light.

Even though I wanted to just throw this all over to the police and let them figure out everything, I had a problem wondering who would've killed Sam. I mean, Sam was the nicest guy I had ever met, and that's how most people looked at him and saw him. He didn't want to hurt a fly unless the fly hurt him. He never made fun of the geeks or the gays or anyone else. He never told a racist joke the entire time I knew him. It just wasn't who he was. He never put anyone down or took anything from anyone. Maybe Sam was secretly gay, and that's why he killed himself. Knowing it would cause a stir...

Oh please... There's no way that's possible. If anyone's gay, it's me for thinking about how much I miss him all the damn time.

No matter... I just didn't know how I would present this idea to Chief Ramzorin:

"So Chief, Ben and I think that Sam was murdered by another student at our school."

"Oh really? Why's that?"

"Because Sam would never commit suicide; it just doesn't make sense."

"Suicide never makes sense, kid, so always remember to live."

That's how I imagined the conversation in my head. But, murder did seem logical for the most part. That would explain why it happened right at the end of the year... so the senior that did it could get away with it easier. After this year, all of the seniors are going to go their separate ways.

They say that after senior year, you only talk to about two or three people that you graduate with for the rest of your life. That seemed hard to believe, especially now that there is Facebook, but whatever. I'll just believe the statistic for now in hopes to prove it wrong eventually.

So, now I narrowed it down to the seniors, and it wasn't me or Ben... so now, the police would have eighty-three people to interview.

They're not going to like me for this proposition.

Driving past the bowling alley, I thought again about how Alyssa and I met there. Sam was just calling a little get together... or wait, no, that's not what happened. They were having what they called a "public anniversary" since they had been dating a year. Yeah... A tiny celebration is what it was... or, was supposed to be. They liked each other all through freshman year, dated all sophomore year, and then celebrated at the beginning of junior year at the bowling alley. Sam said something about being on too many standard dates with Emily, so he wanted to change things up.

"Plus," I remember him saying as we drove to the bowling alley that night in his beat-up Mustang convertible, and the memory came to life as I drove to the police station, "we need to get you a girl, Jack."

"Me? Why do I need a girlfriend so bad? You're sounding like my Mom," I said, and I started talking in a really annoying way just for comedic effect, " 'Jack, honey, you need to get out more often! Jack, the only time you leave the house is to hang out with Sam or to take the trash out for me!' Yeah, that's you right now."

Sam started laughing his signature laugh that he only seemed to do around me. It seemed like if he laughed around other people he was just trying to be nice, or they just couldn't crack him up like I could.

He pulled up into the small parking strip in front of the bowling alley and I started laughing. He looked at me and said, "What?"

"You parked in a handicapped spot!" I shouted, pointing at the sign. "What are you, retarded or something?"

"Hey, don't joke about that," Sam said as we started backing out of the spot. "The only way we'll be parking there again is if you're driving after I poke one of your eyes out for saying that."

"... I'm sorry, Sam," I said after I stopped laughing.

There was a larger parking lot in the back and we headed there next.

It was already pretty packed, and I saw Emily standing outside next to a car. She was wearing a little blue dress that was cut off at the knees and Sam was wearing his dad's old leather football jacket, but he always looked good no matter what. All of the girls thought he was so attractive, but they never said anything about it in front of Emily, except that she was lucky.

"Oh shit," Sam said. "I was supposed to dress up?"

"Well, maybe a little bit of dressing up wouldn't have killed you," I said. Looking back on that, I wish I would've chosen a better phrase.

Anyway, Sam parked at the closest parking spot and we got out of his car to meet with Emily. She ran up to Sam with her arms open and she kissed his lips, not even caring that he didn't dress up at all.

"Hey baby, why aren't you inside?" Sam asked Emily.

"They made me wait out here... I guess Mr. Saitov got a few calls ahead of time to make a little surprise for us; a lot of people are here."

Mr. Saitov was a Russian immigrant whose family had been here since the start of Stanton. He was nice and giving. He never made a problem for anyone, and he always had advice to those willing to listen.

He was a little short and balding with some stray hairs every once in a while to a point where if you wanted to map the hairs on his head, it would just be some random Xs everywhere. His son was just a year behind us and I'd only talked to him once. He seemed nice enough.

"Hi, Jack," Emily said. She looked at me while in Sam's arms.

"Hey, Emily, how's it going?"

"Pretty great! What about you?"

"Oh, just the same old stuff," I answered with a smile.

Before Emily could say anything else, Mr. Saitov walked out of the back entryway of the bowling alley that was for the personnel only and waved at us to come and see everything.

"C'mon! We'll come through the front!" Mr. Saitov shouted with a big grin.

Sam shrugged and we all walked over to Mr. Saitov as he rounded the corner with us and pointed at the front doors. The doors were glass, but they were covered in black parchment paper to hide what was really inside, even though I was pretty sure it was still just the bowling alley.

"Here!" Mr. Saitov suggested as he wiped his hands on his apron to then grab one of Sam's hands and one of Emily's hands, "You grab one door and the Misses can grab the other, and when I say go, you can both open the doors at the same time! But pull really hard!"

As happy as Mr. Saitov was, I thought he must've taken the whole damn day just to set up this little surprise.

Sam put his right hand on the right door handle and Emily grabbed the left door handle with her left hand and I stood awkwardly between them but a little farther back beside Mr. Saitov.

Mr. Saitov glanced at me to make sure I was excited and I smiled back really quickly to show that I was, and then he turned back to Emily and Sam and said, "Okay... Go!"

At that moment, Sam and Emily yanked the doors open and the strings for some poppers appeared on the other side, and there blew the confetti, along with the cheers of the whole damn town. With as small of a town as we were in, everyone heard about the little celebration and decided to come along. Sam didn't mind. In fact, he was ecstatic as he walked in the door and had his fellow football mates grab him and carry him off somewhere. I walked in alongside Mr. Saitov and Emily to see everything. Above us was a huge banner that read, "ONE YEAR, AIN'T THAT SOMETHING?" and I laughed at the simplicity of the idea. Maybe the adults were trying to satire us kids by pointing out that their relationships were longer than a year.

But, no matter. Sam was pulled off to see a cake that was made at the local bakery and Emily was laughing and cheering at the surprise. Mr. Saitov patted Emily's back and said, "You like it?"

Emily nodded with much appreciation and then Mr. Saitov shouted, "Hey everyone: free bowl, free drinks, free everything!"

It was such a mess of things and people, but it was the happiest time since everything had happened with my dad, and I knew this was special for Sam and Emily, two of the nicest kids in town, who I felt honored to know.

Mr. Saitov walked away to stand behind the bar and help anyone who needed bowling shoes or anything else. Eventually, Sam made his way back to Emily and me and more people walked over to talk to us. Travis Porter, Gregory Allen, and Raymond Todd were first since they were all football buddies. They cracked a few jokes at each other and then made harmless passes at Emily.

Doug came over by himself but he was one of the only people I knew who could pull off being by himself and not look completely lonely.

Ben also was there, which was surprising, since his dad usually never let him out in the town after school was over.

Harold, Mark, and Nick even walked over to say hello and congratulations to Sam and Emily, and then hello to me. I just stood there with Sam and Emily at the doorway, waiting for them to make a move. I didn't feel creepy per se, but I knew I was a little out of place.

Then, I saw her, the girl Sam was always mentioning.

Alyssa Jackson.

I knew she was friends with Emily, and that's why she was coming over here. But as she started to, Sam gave me a look of encouragement and said, "You'll like this girl, Jack. Trust me."

I got a little mad and said, "Wait, you already planned this all out, didn't you?"

Before he could answer, Alyssa was in hearing range and she started talking to Emily.

She was wearing a Beatles shirt that showed how big of a chest she had and some tight dark blue jeans… I remember that pretty well, and don't even think of calling me a perv. The fact is, she looked good, and I already liked her for her taste in music. At least, I was hoping it was her taste in music and she wasn't just wearing the shirt because it was cool. One time, I ran into a girl at school, who was rocking the scene style but she had on an AC/DC shirt. So, I asked, "Do you even know who AC/DC is?"

"Sure! Don't they fix downed power lines?"

But that's beside the point.

"Hi Emily, hope you like everything!" Alyssa said.

Emily stepped in to give Alyssa a hug and said, "Oh yes, this is so great! I can't believe so many people came!"

"Well, not much else to do around here I suppose," Alyssa said with a gleaming smile that made me feel hot.

Sam turned over to me and said, "Hey Alyssa, I don't know if you've met my 'bff', Jack."

"No, not up close and personal, but I have heard of you," she replied, and then she looked at me. "Raymond Todd was being a real jerk that day, huh?"

I made a face, a little embarrassed that she knew about that. To me, she seemed like a pacifist who wanted a similar boyfriend, but maybe not.

"Uh… Yeah," I said at a fourth-grade reading level.

She smiled at me, knowing how I felt. I didn't know how to react to everything around me.

Sam decided to pull the final move though, and he said, "Well, I think Emily and I are going to go enjoy this little gathering. I'll leave you and Jack here so he can torture you some more."

Sam winked at me as he put his arm around his girl and whisked her away. Now, I was left alone with a natural beauty that had already turned my face red as a cherry. I only knew that because she said, "Hey, you look like your face is flushed... Do you need something to drink?"

"Oh, no, it's just that uh..."

"Oh, hey Jack, honey!"

That was the moment I thought everything was done for.

My Mom was here.

She walked up to us, a bottle of beer in her hand and a smile on her face.

"I really like your shirt," my Mom said to Alyssa as she approached us, and then looked at me, "Who's this girl, Jack?"

She walked up closer to us and Alyssa didn't hesitate to make herself known.

"Thanks!" Alyssa started, making sure my Mom knew that she heard the comment about her shirt. "And my name's Alyssa, you probably know my grandparents: Tawny and Frank Jackson?"

"Yeah, as a matter of fact, I do know them! They live just a few houses down from us, right Jack? You used to mow their lawn during the summer," my Mom said.

"I remember pretty well, Mom," I said, trying to get her to go away.

Unfortunately, she picked up on my tone of voice and said, "Hey mister, they said this was a public event so I decided to come! If you don't like that, then buzz off!"

She always said her insults in a silly way just to lighten the mood. It worked on Alyssa as she shared a laugh with my mom, but I didn't laugh, and if I did, it was an awkward forced one.

"Well okay kids, I'll leave you alone now. Jack, did you take your underwear out of the dryer before Sam got you?"

"Uh, Mom," I said.

"I'm kidding of course! See you kiddos later," my Mom said, and with that, she walked off.

Alyssa kept laughing, knowing that my Mom had done that on purpose, but luckily, my face started to cool off and I tried to act like that never happened.

"I'm sorry about that," I said.

"No, don't worry. Your Mom seems cool!" Alyssa said. "I wish my Mom was like that... But, I just live with my grandparents now, so it's no big deal."

"Oh, okay," I said, knowing that asking anything more about her living situation would be too far out of bounds for right now.

"So, a drink?" she asked.

"I'll get it myself," I answered.

"Oh, well okay then," Alyssa said, a little hurt.

Desperate to save myself, I said, "I didn't mean it like that... I just think it's wrong to rely on women to get me stuff, you know?"

"Oh!" she said, and that amazing smile reappeared. "That's cool, I like that."

So, for the rest of the enchanting night, we talked and talked and ate and talked and talked and ate some cake and drank some pop and talked some more, to a point where my face never felt all hot around her anymore. We shared funny stories, serious stories, weird stories, stories that were totally random, and some made up just for good measure. My Mom even said bye to me at one point, and I checked my watch to see what time it was. It was pushing eleven o'clock, and I knew that I probably needed to go home too.

Sam and Emily were bowling their lives away, having the time of their lives and sharing a deep kiss after each strike. It seemed like Sam's idea for the public anniversary went off without a hitch. Now, Alyssa and I just watched as they bowled, both too shy to try and bowl in front of each other. Plus, talking to her was so much better.

"I promise you, I haven't bowled in a long time," I said. "If I tried, I'd probably throw the ball into the other lanes."

Alyssa laughed and ate the last French fry in our basket. I was glad that she appreciated the jokes I was making. I couldn't remember the last time I tried getting a girl to like me, but it was pretty long ago.

"Jack, why haven't we hung out more often... or even spoken to each other until now?" Alyssa asked.

"Well I mean, I never really see you at school that often," I said.

"Bull," she replied. "With only eighty-five kids in our class, I'm pretty sure you've seen me before. Actually, I know I've seen you before. We have the same lunch."

"Oh yeah? Well, why haven't you come and talked to me?"

"You were in dude territory. I know what would've happened if I approached you then."

It was back when I used to sit by Sam and a lot of the football players, and although I wasn't a football player, they still accepted me for knowing Sam.

"What would that be?"

"Huh?"

"What would happen if you approached me in 'dude territory'?"

"Oh, let me think… I'm not trying to brag or anything, but I think a few of the guys would whistle and holler and give you a hard time that I came to talk to you."

"Really? What makes you think I wouldn't be the one whistling?" I asked daringly, trying to spark something out of instinct.

Sadly, the moment was postponed when Mr. Saitov started turning off some of the lights, and I realized the only people there were me, Alyssa, Sam, Emily, and Mr. Saitov. Once he turned off a few lights and Sam and Emily's game ended, Mr. Saitov walked over to Alyssa and me and said, "Oh kids, I don't think the free games, free drinks, and free everything was that good of an idea. I think I'm in the hole about five figures now."

"I'll start a fundraiser at the school for you, Mr. Saitov," I said, trying to be generous in a joking way.

"No, it'd really help if you could help me get all this confetti crap off the ground," Mr. Saitov said in a hard tone, but then laughed and said, "I'm kidding of course. You kids need to get on home now, curfew's in about thirty minutes, right?"

"Yes Mr. Saitov, we'll be leaving now," Sam shouted as he stumbled with Emily in his left arm, and then, he caught her off guard by lifting her up. She squealed a little bit as he stepped back onto the regular carpet.

"Hey, you guys didn't get any shoes!" Mr. Saitov complained to Sam and Emily as we started walking out of the bowling alley.

"Yeah, sorry Mr. Saitov, but they're just not stylish enough," Sam said with a grin.

Mr. Saitov waved us on and shook his head and we thanked him for everything before walking out into the intoxicating moonlight. The night seemed young until I yawned so loudly I thought I might just fall asleep right then and there.

"Past your bedtime, Jack?" Sam asked as we stood on the sidewalk about to head for the back parking lot.

"Something like that," I said since nothing clever came to mind.

"Well hey, I think I'm going to take my beautiful girl home now if you don't mind. Jack, do you need a ride home?"

"No, don't worry about it, Sam," Alyssa stepped in. "I'm going to take Jack home if he doesn't have a car."

Sam raised his eyebrows at me in a suggestive way and said, "Oh okay, yeah, sure, if you don't mind."

"I sure don't," Alyssa said, pulling a set of keys out of her pocket that I didn't even know could fit in her jeans... I'm trying to say they were so tight.

"Well, ¡adios amigos!" Sam said, and with that, he walked toward the back parking lot carrying Emily, leaving Alyssa and me alone.

After we watched them walk off, I turned to Alyssa and she said, "Okay kid, let's go to my car. It's just across the street."

After she pointed it out, we jaywalked across the street and I got on the passenger side of her red Hyundai minivan and she unlocked the doors with her remote. Once I got in, she did too and started the car before even closing her door. With a slam, she closed her door and I closed mine too. A little quicker than I wanted to, she pulled away from the curb and I struggled to put my seatbelt on.

"You're different," Alyssa said.

"How?" I asked, finally getting my seatbelt on and bumping up my chances of survival by eighty percent.

"Well, I left the topic of my parents kinda vague, and you haven't asked about them."

"For the same reason you don't mention my dad," I replied slyly.

"Touché," Alyssa said. "But, just so we're honest with each other, my parents weren't very good to me. My Dad insisted on making my life a living hell, and I'm not just saying that because I'm a teenager, I mean he really did make it a living hell. I don't really want to go into details on that..."

"You don't have to," I said, spotting her change of mood from good to bad.

"Okay, good," she said. "But, what about your Dad, if you don't mind me asking?"

I was a little surprised that she did, but I didn't think she was going to use the information in a bad way, so I told her.

"My Dad was killed in Iraq two years ago by an IED, which is an improvised explosive device. There were two of them, one in a car on each side of the road. When they defused one, they set off the other, which is the one my Dad was standing by, making sure no one else came to mess with it. It killed four soldiers, and one was my Dad..."

"Hey, I'm sorry, you didn't have to tell me..."

"No, don't worry. The only other person I've talked about it with was Sam."

Alyssa took a glance at me just to see if I really was okay, and then she asked, "You and Sam are really close, aren't you guys?"

"Yeah, we are," I said, not making it too corny. "We're like brothers, but without all the random fights and annoyances."

"That's good," she replied.

Pretty soon after that, we arrived at my house which was barely lit up by the porch light and garage light; a two-story house, with my bedroom window looking right at us. She pulled up right next to the curb and didn't hit my mailbox, which was good. That would make my Mom like her more. But when she put the car in park, I was a little surprised that she knew right where my house was and it gave me the creeps.

"So... Do you come here often or something?" I asked, taking off my seatbelt as she turned off her headlights.

"Not often enough," Alyssa replied, and my mind started to race with all kinds of thoughts and feelings no one could control.

"Oh, well uh, maybe we could hang out sometime soon," I said, trying to get my composure back.

"Yeah, we should," she replied.

"Okay..." I said; a little scared of what would happen next. "I should go inside now, but thanks for the ride."

I started to step out, but she didn't even respond. Instead, she just kept staring at me with hauntingly beautiful hazel eyes. It was hard not to look back at her, or look away, hell, everything was "hard".

That's when for the first time in my life, I decided to do what I wanted to do right when I wanted to do it. She was staring at me for a reason, and I knew that. I knew this wasn't as innocent as I thought it was in the beginning. No, no, this was something bigger, something unexpected. She wanted me to kiss her, so I gave it to her.

Without fully thinking it through, I leaned in with one arm pulling her in closer, and I gave her the best kiss I could've produced from my dry lips. Her lip's moisture kept us at equilibrium though, and we held the kiss for about fifteen or twenty seconds until I finally pulled away and she looked blown away.

"Goodnight, Alyssa," I said, trying to keep it cool.

And then, keeping my composure, I stepped out toward my lawn, and I...

Tripped.

Tripped and fell, right onto my face into the dew that was just starting to form in the grass.

Somehow, my foot had stepped onto the curb and wasn't completely balanced because I was trying to look cool and stay cool and get the hell out of there before I messed everything up, although I did, or at least, I thought I did.

Alyssa jumped out of the driver's seat, her car still running, and she ran over to check on me. I didn't want to lift my face up from the grass, but I ended up doing it anyway because her hands insisted to.

"Oh my God!" she started as she knelt down beside me and started lifting my head off of the grass. I turned my head to look at her and she actually looked really scared and worried. "Are you okay? I pulled up as close to the curb as I could, I promise!"

But from all of her fear for nothing, I started laughing, slowly at first, but in time, it grew more and more and she actually joined in laughing, knowing that I was okay and that everything would be okay...

HONK!

Looking in my rearview mirror, I saw that now, back in real life, I had been sitting at a green light just daydreaming about that day a year and a half ago. The old man flailed his arm out the window and yelled something at me that I couldn't make out, but I decided to just hit the gas instead of worrying about what he called me.

Jesus, maybe I do miss Alyssa...

*****

At the police station, nothing was really going on. I parked in the civilian parking zone which was pretty small, and I walked straight in through the front doors.

An African American woman stood at the front desk, making sure everyone knew where to go. When I walked in, looking at the pictures overhead of previous chiefs of police spanning through the town's history, the lady looked at me and said, "Oh, Jack, dear, I'm so sorry about what happened. Go on back; they'll be glad to help you."

I thanked her, not knowing completely how she knew my name. Maybe Chief Ramzorin told her beforehand that I might stop by.

The other section of the police station was blocked off by a cedar door that was almost darker than the African American woman at the front desk. Once I stepped through, I saw a few things that didn't surprise me, but I didn't mean it in an offensive way, there just wasn't much crime, and that's why the police officers were mostly sitting around. This was one of those towns where the authorities were mostly called on the fact that a cat was stuck in a tree at the park which was in Forest Haven.

The four cops I saw standing around were just drinking some water from the cooler on the right side of the room, with a Keurig coffee maker on the table next to it. At the very far end of the room, I saw Chief Ramzorin's office and I made my way over to it. The cops didn't even give me much attention; they probably knew why I was here.

The blinds on Chief Ramzorin's windows and door were closed most of the way, so I knew I'd have to knock first. But just before I did…

"Hey, Jack, whatcha doin'? Did you take care of my good-for-nothing cousin for me?"

I turned to the left to see Donovan Young standing there in a cheap suit drinking some morbidly black coffee. I wasn't too surprised to see him there since there aren't ever any murders in Stanton. I had one to give him, but I'd rather run it by Chief Ramzorin first.

"Oh, I'm just here to see the Chief," I said.

"Well he's on the phone with the mayor," Donovan replied. His greased back hair stood untouched by any other elements. "Is there something I can help you with?"

"Eh… No offense," I said, trying to deliver it as lightly as possible, "but I'd rather talk to Chief Ramzorin."

"Hey, not telling me is obstruction of justice," Donovan said, feeling cool because he knew some fancy terms to throw at me. "How about you just tell me?"

"I just don't feel comfortable telling you," I said.

"C'mon Jack, I helped you when you wrecked your bicycle on the Stanton Stretch and cried your eyes out about ten years ago."

"Hah, still holding that against me, huh?"

"If I have to," Donovan said.

Before Donovan could get my story out of me, Chief Ramzorin stepped out of his office and looked right at me.

"Huh, I knew that was your voice, Jack," the Chief said. "Come on in."

Right when I thought I had won against Donovan, the Chief also signaled for him to come in with us.

Donovan: 1, Me: 0.

When we both walked in, the Chief signaled for me to take a seat across from his seat and I did. Donovan remained standing and watched over me.

"So, Jack," Chief Ramzorin started. "Is something on your mind?"

"Uh, yes sir, that's quite an understatement actually," I said.

"Oh really? Well go ahead son, tell me what's on your mind?"

I hated when people called me son, besides my Mom. Once in ninth grade, right when everything had happened, my baseball coach called me that and I cried for the rest of the game. I probably sound like a wimp for crying so much, but you don't understand. Nobody does.

"Well," I said, taking a glance over at Donovan to see if he was even paying attention, but he was. "Chief, I know this might sound crazy, but my friend and I have been thinking, and we believe that Sam didn't commit suicide, but it was murder."

I heard Donovan almost spit out his coffee and the Chief looked at me with a scorned face.

"What!? Murder? Here, in Stanton?"

"I know it's crazy, but..."

"Look, Jack, I hate to say this, and I know you're going through a rough time right now, but it was definitely suicide. Trust us on this," Chief Ramzorin guaranteed in a melancholy way.

"No, Chief, you don't understand," I begged. "I'm not saying that you didn't do your job well or anything like that, I'm just saying, well, suicide just doesn't make sense, sir. Sam wouldn't do something like that."

"Let me tell you something, Jack," the Chief said in a fatherly tone, ready to cut down the whole idea. "Sometimes, we think we know people really well, but we actually don't know them at all. Sometimes, you have to think that everyone in the world has two sides, and that's not always a bad thing, as long as you get one side to like you more than the other, if the other side is ugly. I agree, suicide is strange for a kid like Sam. He was nice, caring, loving, a great athlete; had a great girlfriend… But maybe that ugly side just got the best of him, and he couldn't take it anymore. You know, even though popular kids are so popular, sometimes they become that way just to cover up all of their shortcomings. I hate to tell you all of this, Jack, but you're an adult now, and you need to know these things for the future, okay?"

I did hate to hear what he had to say, but maybe he was right. I had an ugly side, and it came out the moment Sam killed himself. But that didn't mean I was going to kill myself because of that ugly side, it just meant that I needed to get back to the good side of things.

"But, out of curiosity," Donovan said, cutting into the conversation. "Who do you think would kill Sam?"

"I… don't have any suggestions off the top of my head, but I'm pretty sure it'd be a student in my grade."

"And what makes you say that?"

"Well, it's senior year, and it's almost the end of the year, so if they got away with the murder so far, then maybe they'd really get away with it forever, since we're all going to split and go our separate ways after this year."

"You need a little more understanding on police work and investigations, but you have a good point," Donovan said, almost sounding like he was on my side about the whole thing.

"Yes, but not something we should actually pursue, okay?" Chief Ramzorin requested. "Jack, if you do find out something though, or you know something else, you know you can tell us, right?"

"Yeah, I know that," I said. "You gave me your card; I know how to get a hold of you."

"That's good, Jack," Chief Ramzorin ended with a small smile, and he decided to change the subject with the usual, "I hope school was okay for you, was it?"

"Yes, it was, thanks," I said, and I stood up to leave the station.

"Need Donovan to help you see your way out?" Chief Ramzorin asked.

"No, that's okay," I said, and then, I made my way back to my car and back home.

*****

After dinner, once I had finished talking to my Mom and cleared my plate, I went up to my room and texted Ben, telling him the police idea was no dice. He texted back, saying, "Damn, well maybe we need to just accept the loss and move on. They would know if it was suicide. We'll get through this, Jack."

His willingness to give up surprised me, and that's when my crazy hormones made me think of a plan.

I texted him back.

"No, I'm not going to accept that Sam committed suicide. He was murdered, and I'll find who did it."

After that, I turned my phone off for the night and plugged it into the wall charger. Ben probably thought I was crazy, but he made me this way, by proposing that Sam didn't commit suicide, but instead, was murdered by one of our fellow classmates.

But why would someone kill Sam? Who would kill Sam?

The craziness led to paranoia and I walked over to my shoebox that had memories of my dad. I remembered a gift he had once given me, back in seventh grade when he came back home for a few months before leaving again. It was a Special Forces pocket knife with a good grip on it. I remembered playing around with it as soon as I got it, but my Mom took it away from me. After Dad's funeral, she gave it back, saying I was more mature now and she felt bad for keeping it.

I let the knife come out a little bit, and then, with a flick of the wrist, I let the knife come out and I held it in a stance.

Whoever killed Sam might not have just wanted to kill Sam, maybe they wanted to kill me too, especially if I start looking for them.

That was the whole reason I got the knife. And when I took my shirt off and changed into some pajama pants, I slipped into bed, holding the knife in my right hand, and just as I closed my eyes, I promised something that I'd never turn back on.

I'm going to find who killed you, Sam...

Chapter Four
The Investigation
The Sampson Residence
Tuesday, May 22nd
7:30 am

The next morning I was right back at school, but with new intentions and new goals.

But before heading there, at breakfast my Mom noticed I was a little jittery without even drinking any coffee and she actually sat down to talk to me before she left for work, since she had to make a thirty-minute drive every morning to Detroit.

My Mom was an accountant at some law firm that was just barely making it. She worried about losing her job every day, and I hadn't thought about it much until she started talking to me again.

"Honey, you okay?" she asked lightly.

"Yeah, Mom, I'm all right," I answered.

She scooted a chair over closer to me and sat down to rub my shoulders.

"I heard about... what happened at the funeral," my Mom said, bringing it up as lightly as possible.

"Yeah, I'm okay, Mom," I said, choking up a little bit.

Once she realized that she was upsetting me even more, she changed the subject and asked, "You look hyped up, something going on at school?"

"Eh, I don't know yet. Maybe I'll find out when I get there," I replied.

My left leg bounced up and down silently under the table and I tried finishing my Cheerios before they all got soggy.

My Mom leaned in to hug me, and I tried to return it, but it was one of those awkward hugs where someone comes in from behind and you end up just patting their arms.

"When I get home tonight, I'll make us a great dinner, okay? Just you and me, no more fast food."

"Yeah, Mom, that sounds good," I said faintly.

"Okay, and I want to talk to you tonight a little more, if you don't mind."

"Don't we usually?"

"Sometimes, but I know you're upset and this is a hard time for you, but soon you'll cope with this loss in some way and we can move on to greater things," my Mom said, not really sure how to give a motivational speech.

"Sure, Mom, let's hope so," I said.

She kissed me on the back of the head, and with the clacking of her heels, she was out the door.

*****

In the nick of time, I made it to school just as the first bell was ringing. Joey and his friends headed up to the school and I shut off my engine to trail behind them so they wouldn't talk to me.

I was hoping I wouldn't be late. For some reason, talking to my Mom sort of slowed me down and I ended up brushing my teeth for about ten minutes straight. The Listerine in the toothpaste burned my gums to a new level of pain, but I didn't even really think about it or feel it until I came to my senses.

The same thing happened when my Dad passed on, or was taken away from me. I think that's a better way to put it. I took a forty-five-minute shower, when I usually just took a ten-minute shower. My Mom ended up knocking on the door as hard as she could, since I didn't hear her the first few times. That's when I remember looking up and being blinded by the shower water… I ended up sitting on the drain and just letting the water depress me even more.

But throwing those thoughts aside, and hoping that I could find out something about Sam's murder today, I tried to stay as positive as I possibly could, but murder wasn't positive.

Checking my pockets, I had my phone, but I didn't turn it back on yet. When I did, I saw fourteen new texts… wow.

All from random people, most of them were numbers I didn't even have saved in my phone yet. The only one I paid attention to was the response to the text I sent Ben last night. He said, "What? Are you gonna be a detective now? Maybe it's time Donovan's spot was taken over."

I scoffed, thinking about how Ben was trying to be funny. But, he was right. I was playing detective, but it wasn't really a game for me.

*****

First hour: English IV. I made it just in time, and Ben glanced over at me when I walked in, trying to show concern for me not answering his text message last night. I sort of ignored him though, and sat down in my seat as soon as the late bell rang.

*****

Second hour: Calculus I. In that class, I started thinking about who would kill Sam, since Mr. Harrison was sharing some funny story that he told at the beginning of the year, but I was the only student who cared enough to remember it.

Who would kill Sam? What student here at Stanton High would even really think about doing it, unless they themselves were high on something? That seemed to be the only logical way that someone would kill Sam.

Thinking back on old detective shows, I started by thinking of what their motive would be.

Well… Sam didn't have the power to really screw anyone over, or the reputation of doing something like that.

Maybe… a grudge? An old grudge?

But for some reason, my mind just didn't think about it seriously.

Yeah, Jack, someone's pissed at Sam for taking their swing back in elementary, or not letting them on the Merry-Go-'Round.

It made me mad that I couldn't think seriously about it, but see, that's the problem from the beginning. It didn't make any sense that Sam would commit suicide, and it almost makes sense to a negative point of someone killing Sam.

What the hell…

Oh well, maybe I shouldn't try and make up a motive just yet. I needed to talk to someone, someone that was closer to Sam than I was…

Emily.

*****

Third hour, Sociology, seemed to fly by pretty quickly. All I did was study the society that lay before me in the classroom. Today, no one gave a crap about Sam. Gregory Allen didn't even care to mention him or anything like that. Instead, Mr. Tinley just said we had to write down ten facts over a video about Phineas Gage and his attitude after being stabbed through the head by a railway spike that shot up from the ground. Right now, I wouldn't really mind if that happened to me.

*****

Fourth hour, Government, I walked in hoping to see Emily and start asking her some questions, but instead, she wasn't here.

51

I walked up to Miss Evans, who seemed pretty occupied with something on her computer. I didn't care that I'd interrupt it.

"Miss Evans?" I started.

Her eyes kept flying around on the computer screen and she didn't even bother to look at me, or even acknowledge that I said anything. But just as I started to speak again, she said, "Hold on just a second…"

I waited, not really sure what she was doing on her computer. For all I know, she was either playing the Impossible Game or watching some cat video on YouTube.

"Okay, Jack, what is it?" she asked as she turned away from staring at her computer screen.

She lifted her little rectangular glasses off the bridge of her nose and let them rest at the top of her chest since she tied yarn around the ends. Her face was veiny and she was very thin, to a point where even the cheerleaders knew they couldn't achieve it.

"Uh, do you know where Emily is?" I asked.

"No, not off the top of my head," she replied.

"Well… The late bell rang a few minutes ago, could you check?" I asked nicely.

"Well, where would I check? By looking over at her desk, I can see she isn't present, therefore…"

"Maybe someone sent you an email about where she is," I suggested, already tired of her game.

"There's a good suggestion," she said, and she began fiddling around on her computer again. I just hope it didn't take as long as last time.

Soon enough, she pulled up an email and said, "You know, I don't even know why you asked if I knew since you knew that there'd be an email. It's from the counselor, saying she'll be in there all hour."

"Oh," I said, a little surprised. Usually, Emily was just late because she took so long on tests, but now that I thought about it, we didn't have any more tests… Silly me I guess.

"Okay, thanks, Miss Evans," I said.

As I started walking back to my seat, everyone else in class was talking to one another and not really recognizing me, but that's what I wanted right now.

Except, then I saw one lone pair of eyes staring me down, and I wondered how long he'd been looking at me.

Oliver Pinkerton, one of the kids that was lower in popularity but I didn't know why. I guess he had just a few pimples too many to be a pretty boy.

He sat in front of me, and he flipped his hair out of the way before talking to me.

"Hey, Jack, what's up?" he asked.

"Nothing really, just checking on Emily," I responded.

"Yeah, I was actually going to tell you, she asked Mr. Davis last hour if she could leave to talk to the counselor, and he said okay. Is she all right?"

"As good as she can be I suppose."

"And what about you?"

I sat down, not really crazy about the question, but I'd answer it to be polite. Before this, it seemed like he had only asked me for paper on assignments.

"To be honest with you, Oliver, I'm pretty damn terrible."

Miss Evans head perked up, knowing she had heard a curse word, but didn't know exactly where it came from, so she looked back down at her computer.

Oliver noticed that she looked over and he laughed quietly, but then went serious and said, "I know it's hard, man. My cousin killed himself over credit card debt and student loans a few years ago that just kept mounting up and up and up until he couldn't take it anymore."

Sam didn't have credit cards though…

I would've passed by the theory of murder to him, but I didn't want to have it spread around and scare off the killer… or maybe I should just say, possible killer.

"Did you go to Shakey's after the funeral?"

"Yeah, I did. Hannah Carlisle invited me, so I tagged along with her."

"Were you worried about me since I didn't go?"

"Oh, no man, I understood completely. Now Alyssa on the other hand…"

"Yeah, I already heard all about that," I said, not too pleased, but glad that someone finally didn't think I was going to kill myself just because my best friend did.

"Yeah…" Oliver said, not really sure how to transition to something else, so he didn't. "You know what man, can I run something by you really quickly, but I don't want it to upset you."

"Don't worry about it, just say it," I said, not sure what to expect.

"Well, you see Jack, I've noticed today… Well, just look at these people," Oliver said, pointing to the other students in the room.

I looked around in the room, seeing what he was talking about almost immediately, but I let him explain at the same time.

"Yesterday, it was all just a big depress fest, to say the least. Sam's suicide was something that everyone was thinking about and dreading. But now, it's just a new fuckin' day, and they don't seem to have a care in the world about Sam, or what happened to him. Maybe they can just cope better than you and me and Emily, or they just didn't care in the first place. It's a sickening thought, but you just have to roll with it I guess."

Oliver's depressing words made me not feel like the only person who cared anymore, but at the same time, Oliver was never really one to shed a bunch of sadness on a situation, so I started to worry about him. But, my worries were halted when I thought about how he didn't worry about me when I didn't go to Shakey's, so I paid him the same respect.

With Oliver's new point of view now out in the open, I wondered if I should tell him the murder theory. No… It was best not to. Plus, I was interrupted by kooky Miss Evans as she finally announced almost halfway through the class, "Oh, your assignment is up front. It's due at the end of the hour."

*****

Fifth hour, Humanities, I walked in hoping maybe Emily would be here, but she wasn't. Not yet, anyway.

Doug greeted me at the door, not as optimistic as yesterday.

"Hi, Jack," Doug said with no tone.

"Hey, Doug, don't hit your head on the doorway on the way out," I replied.

It happened once before, but I couldn't remember where. Maybe it was on the school bus.

Doug flashed me a short and sweet smile before leaving to go wherever he needed to go. I walked in, not really sure how I was presenting myself, but people still weren't staring at me like the day before, or at Sam's depressingly empty desk. Instead, just like the hour before, everyone was talking about different things and laughing and celebrating a close end to the year; discussing future plans, asking each other if they could rent apartments together, even though it was just speculation, and, on top of it all, some party was being organized for after graduation. Not being my type of thing, I strayed away from their conversation and headed for my desk.

Class started and Emily still wasn't back. Her empty seat sat before me and I wondered when she would get back.

There, right in the open, sat Alyssa. She hadn't talked to me at all today, maybe since I bit her head off yesterday. I felt bad about it now, and realized it was the first thing I had cared about besides Sam's suicide, or now, murder.

I leaned forward, deciding to exchange a few words with Alyssa before Miss Hannah started the class.

"Alyssa," I said, trying to keep it down, knowing that all the other students would pounce at the idea that I might be asking her out.

But, she didn't turn around. Instead, she stared forward, running her fingers through her hair, and I felt like she was ignoring me on purpose.

I leaned in more, but I was just glad no one sat behind me, otherwise, my butt would be right in their face, and I whispered harshly, "Alyssa!"

Finally, she turned around, and I hadn't made a scene yet. My butt went back into my chair and I motioned for her to sit in Emily's seat, since we didn't have assigned seats. Not according to Miss Hannah anyway.

Alyssa stood up, a little surprised by my offer, but she walked over to the desk and sat down, facing me head on.

"What is it?" Alyssa asked.

"Emily's still with the counselor?" I inquired.

"Yeah, I guess so... She just got really upset in third hour, almost on the verge of crying."

"Oh... Will she be back for lunch?"

"Maybe. Want me to text you if she is?"

"Yeah, that'd be good. I need to talk to her."

Alyssa gave me a funny look, and I hoped she wasn't thinking what I thought she was...

"Oh, well why?"

"It's kinda hard to explain right now..."

"Can't you try? I mean, even if you do talk to her at lunch, I always sit right beside her, outside by the big oak tree in the front, so I'll hear what you say anyway."

I noticed what she was getting at, so I played along.

"Okay then, you can just wait till lunch to find out what I have to say," I retorted.

And before she could argue with me, Miss Hannah announced that she was putting on a video and we all turned to watch it.

*****

I didn't retain any knowledge from the video, except that Da Vinci might have invented the first machine gun, which seemed odd. But once we were released for lunch, I headed for the lunch line, but this time I had to wait, which I didn't mind. I didn't really expect for those kids to keep letting me cut all year long. It was just a one-time token of gratitude to keep me in a good mood, but it didn't work.

I smelled fat and grease back in the kitchen, and I wasn't sure if it was the food or just the workers. I thought about maybe sharing that joke with someone in line, but I decided not to. The only person I usually did that with was Sam, but he wasn't here.

After getting my usual turkey sandwich, I left the room smelling like grease and fat and headed into the commons full of makeup and sarcasm. I saw Harold's table first, and they were quietly talking about something, even though I don't know why I say something, I should just go ahead and say some video game. Next, I saw Ben at the Asian table. I always wondered what it would be like to sit there, and stir up what was the usual protocol.

But I couldn't today, because I felt the jab from my phone vibrating and I knew it was Alyssa telling me that Emily was back. Both Alyssa and Emily always brought their lunches, so I knew they were already at the oak tree out front. Sad thing was, I'd have to walk through the whole damn school just to get there to the front office and see them, but it'd be worth it.

After the insignificant commute to the other side of the school, I stepped outside to be greeted by the sun, who I thought was just messing with me and blinding me to get on my nerves. But once my eyes adjusted, I saw the two lonely girls with broken hearts sitting by the oak tree eating their petite lunches and barely saying anything to each other. Sadly, I'd have to be the one to break their hearts even more.

Emily rubbed at one of her eyes when I walked up. I didn't think I was a tear jerker though, I just think she wanted to make sure she looked presentable, even though she always did.

She looked up at me; a small smile appeared. Alyssa sat there, trying to act like she didn't notice me, even though I saw her look over at me right when I came outside.

"Hi, Jack," Emily started.

"Hey, Emily, and Alyssa," I said, trying to be nice. "How was the counselor?"

"Hah, I feel dumb for even going in the first place," Emily said, and then elaborated. "She doesn't understand what's going on... I guess I shouldn't expect her to."

"I think Principal Leonard is more on our side than anyone else here," I suggested. "He talked to me at the funeral and acted like I could see him anytime. I'm sure the same goes for you."

"Maybe next time, huh?" Emily said with her beautiful smile fading into something darker.

I was glad my upcoming theory didn't have to be the only thing to make her smile disappear.

"So, why'd you come by? Just worried about me?" Emily asked innocently.

"Yeah, that, and I had something to run by you," I added, trying to stall as much as possible before unveiling the incredulous news.

"It's weird," Emily said, making my time to warm up a little longer. "This reminds me of when you two were dating. That's the only other time you'd come see her at lunch."

Alyssa had an awkward look on her face that I'm sure I shared with her, and she said, "Emily, Jack wants to tell you something."

"Oh, yeah, what is it?" Emily asked.

Her eyes showed me that she had no idea what I was about to say, and I regretted the fact that she didn't know. Maybe I should've hinted at it earlier.

"It's about Sam," I started.

Emily scoffed.

"When isn't it?"

"Hah, I know what you mean, but this is a little different."

Emily's head perked up in a scared way and she made me not want to tell her anymore, but I had to if I wanted to try and find who did it.

"Well, not a little different, but a lot... What if I said that Sam didn't commit suicide?"

Emily's face contorted in a way I didn't know was humanly possible. A sick feeling went all over my body and she asked, "What!? What do you mean? This isn't a joke, Jack."

Alyssa was also staring at me in a weird way, but I decided to continue.

"Look, it's not a joke, and I'd never treat it like one. But Ben and I were talking yesterday after school, and we just don't think it could be suicide. So, we concluded that it might be… murder."

The word "murder" slipped out of my mouth and made a mess of everyone's emotions. I tried to keep cool, but Emily made it hard.

"Murder? Why the hell would you even think it could be something like that!?" she shouted.

It was the first time I had ever heard her cuss, and I started to worry that I might've started a fire in this puny forest town.

"Think about it, Emily," I said, being a little more aggressive. "Why in God's name would Sam kill himself like that? He had no reason to. And even if he did, he would've left us a suicide note instead of just making a big mystery out of it. Sam wasn't conceited like that."

The tears of perpetual anguish started to form in Emily's eyes and she argued with me.

"Jack, even if someone did kill Sam, they had no reason to! You and I both know that. Goddammit, I thought maybe I could cope with the idea of suicide, but now murder? Screw off, Jack."

Just as Emily's tears began falling out of her eyes, she ran off before I could grab her and try to say some comforting words. I stood there, feeling like a jackass. Everything was changed now, and not even close to being for the better.

"Why would you even think about that, Jack?"

Alyssa's voice cut into my thoughts and I looked down at her. She was now standing, trying to threaten me with her stance.

I shook my head, feeling stupid and like my emotions had gotten the best of me. Just like with Phineas Gage, but without a hole in my head.

"I don't have time for your condescension," I said, wanting to walk away from the situation. My heartbeat escalated and I didn't want to be here anymore.

"Wait, just tell me. Why would you think someone would kill Sam?" Alyssa asked, now sounding like she wanted to help.

"The same reason it doesn't make sense that he'd kill himself," I answered coldly. "Now I've already talked to the police about the theory but they don't want to help, so now I'm looking, but I'm not doing a very good job."

"Jack," she started delicately, "you can't just run a one-manned investigation."

"I'm not. Ben's helping me too. And I'm only making it small because I don't want to scare off the killer."

"You think it's someone in the school?" Alyssa asked. Worried was the best way to describe her tone.

"I suspect someone in our grade," I corrected.

"Oh my God…"

I felt like now was a good time to walk off before I had to see another girl ball her eyes out in front of me, so I started walking off…

"Wait, Jack."

I stopped, just because I still had past feelings interfering with everything else.

I turned to face her, and her stance was less threatening now.

"I mean, I don't think it's a completely bogus idea that Sam was murdered, but it's just…"

"Do you know someone who could've done it?" I asked with high hopes.

"No… not off the top of my head. But, I do want to help you… and Ben."

"Just keep this between us, okay? That'll help the most," I said.

With that, the bell rang to announce the end of lunch and I walked away from Alyssa without saying a formal goodbye, but she didn't say one either.

*****

In sixth hour, Chemistry II, I found myself deeply regretting even mentioning murder to Emily or Alyssa, but maybe they knew more about investigating than I did. That might be a help, or would it just complicate everything?

I knew if I had a team of Ben, Emily, and Alyssa, emotions would run high the entire time, and cause a fog on the main objective of finding the killer. Or maybe, looking at myself from the outside, I was covered in fog.

Miss Klein questioned my welfare as soon as I walked in the door.

"Yeah, I'm okay," I answered, a little uncomfortable that a teacher cared so much. I wonder why that is…

"Well Jack, if you ever need anything, or someone to talk to, or need to leave for a little bit, let me know."

I wanted to laugh at the idea of a teacher being okay with truancy, but I knew she meant to go talk to the counselor or something.

"Thanks, Miss Klein."

*****

The rest of sixth hour was a breeze, and helped me transition into seventh hour, Journalism, which was also a breeze. Same assignment: Read an article from a newspaper or magazine and write a little summary of it. Somehow, it never got old.

But halfway through the class as I was daydreaming about different things after finishing my assignment, the overhead intercom abruptly came on, calling me down to see Principal Leonard. Mrs. Waverly accepted the request, and I was told to go there redundantly by Mrs. Waverly.

My heart sank. I was dreading the idea of Emily telling on me, or spilling the beans about this whole "investigation", or lack thereof, to Principal Leonard.

"Now Jack, Miss Harper tells me you've gone insane," I could imagine him saying.

I started to walk to the office with heavy feet, but Billy stopped me at the doorway.

"Hey man, are you okay?" Billy asked.

"Yeah dude, I'm fine. Principal Leonard just wants to check on me I guess," I said.

"Well, if you need anything, I'm here," Billy said.

I thanked him and made my way to the office once again, but this time, a thought shot through my head that made me feel old.

This might be the last time I'm ever called up to the office...

For some reason, the thought branched from that to the first day of ninth grade at the high school, back when I was just one of Sam's fanboys and not an actual friend.

We walked in together, and by "we" I mean me, Billy, and Gary, the funny guy. Ahead of us not too far away was Sam, along with his football buddies. Sam was still a good guy, even back then. I guess you could say that he matured physically all the time, but was always fully matured mentally.

For some reason, Billy, Gary, and I were kind of scared of the thought of being at a new school. Sixth grade seemed like a piece of cake transition from the elementary to the middle school, now looking back in hindsight. I guess we were just scared because of some stupid rumor that the older kids might pick on us or beat us up, because the older kids were assholes.

But that day, on the first day of ninth grade, after walking in behind Sam, I didn't fear anything when he turned and saw me cowering with Billy and Gary. And instead of making fun of us, Sam smiled and said, "Don't worry kids, I'll save you if any trouble arises."

Just then, Sam ran into an open locker that Emily was using. She shuddered as Sam's football friends continued on laughing at his demise, and as Sam covered his slowly bleeding nose, Emily reached for a tissue and handed it to him. I guess that's how they started off liking each other.

As for the movie theater, and how we started as friends: Well, I didn't really tell the whole story, so I guess I will now. What really happened was, a few of my friends, i.e. Billy and Gary, had been invited to see some PG-13 POS horror movie by Sam's friends the summer before tenth grade, but after Billy and Gary invited me and I started heading that way, they told me last minute they couldn't make it. I guess they didn't want to be seen with me and my terrible haircut.

So, my Mom dropped me off at the movie because I didn't want to look like a loser in front of her, and I just went on in, acting like everything was good and going right. I stood out in the lobby at first, trying to look like I just didn't know what movie to see after I noticed that Sam and his friends weren't in the movie either. But after a while, to my surprise, Sam walked in alone with his keys dangling from his right hand and a confused look on his face.

But once he saw me, everything clicked.

"Hey," Sam said, and I was surprised he even acknowledged I was there. "Did you get ditched too? Michael and Gregory said they were coming, but now I can't get an answer from either of them."

"Yeah, actually, same thing happened with Billy and Gary," I replied, acting like I wasn't cool with the situation. But I was, since Sam was there.

"Well..." Sam started, and I worried what he'd say next. "Do you wanna see the movie anyway?"

"I don't know... I heard it sucks," I said.

"Well, I didn't drive out here to be stood up, so c'mon," Sam said in an inviting way.

During the movie, I remember laughing and commenting on how stupid it was with Sam. All of my comments and jokes made him laugh, and he seemed to think I was a genius for pointing it all out.

And after the movie ended, the infamous theater fight happened between Sam and me and the kids from a few cities over, just because of my stupid haircut. But Sam insisted that we didn't back down from the fight. For some reason, he had confidence that I was a fighter, but I never learned why…

Anyway, there's that story. Just some fairytale now, or at least, that's what it felt like. It was all just some great dream that satisfied my loss of friends and my Dad…

Walking into the office, only one secretary remained. She just nodded at me and pointed toward Principal Leonard's office as she talked on the phone to a parent and filled out a leaving pass for another student. She knew why I was there.

Principal Leonard's door was just cracked open, and I lightly pushed it and knocked to see what was going on.

"Yes, come in."

Doing as he said, I walked into his office and saw him standing by his window, watching as some kid waiting for his older brother to get released played around on the big oak tree. I didn't know if Principal Leonard was scared for the kid or wanted something to happen.

When I stepped in though, he glanced over and said, "Oh, good, Jack, close the door and sit down."

Following orders again, I did what he said and made myself comfortable in the leather chair that was set before his desk. Once I sat down, he pulled his rolling chair across the wood tile and sat down slowly, as if he was checking for a tack in his chair.

"You wanted to see me?" I asked, almost sounding like some overworked adult.

"Yes," Principal Leonard said.

"Look, if this is about Emily, I didn't mean to upset her…"

"Oh no, she said it wasn't your fault, whatever it was," Principal Leonard said, and I felt relieved because she hadn't told him my crazy theory. "But since she is still broken up pretty bad, which I didn't expect for her to get over it very soon or anything… You get what I mean, right?"

I nodded.

"Good. Well, Jack, I just wanted to see how you were. It surprised me that you came to school Monday, but when I looked on your attendance overall, I saw that you came back the day after your Dad's funeral."

"Yeah… I just don't like to dwell on things for more than I feel is necessary. I mean, I still miss my Dad and I sure as hell miss Sam… Oh, sorry for cussing, sir."

"Forget about it, Jack, you're an adult now, and there are only seven days, almost six days of school left, so I could give less of a damn."

With that, we shared a nice laugh that made me feel a little more comfortable around Principal Leonard. Maybe he wasn't so bad.

"So, Jack, how are things?"

"Are you kidding me?" I asked, not trying to sound too harsh.

"Well I mean, are you making the best of things or can you not sleep at night?"

"I can sleep at night, but for some reason, which I told the counselor this a while back, I don't dream after these tragic events happen," I shared.

"Really?"

"Yeah. If I dream, it's just black. That's all I remember."

"Funny," Principal Leonard said. And afterward, he randomly started to tell me, "Last night I had a dream where me and an old buddy of mine, one I haven't talked to in years, went fishing on some crazy expensive yacht that I would never be able to even set a foot on, and as we fished, he turned on me by pulling a little plug in the hull of the ship, and letting it start to sink. I even laughed in the dream at the fact that it was so silly that the yacht had a little plug just like a little tugboat, you know? Ha-ha. Also, I was surprised to see someone close to me was turning his back on me and screwing me over like that because there was only one life jacket and he took it! Jumped off the boat and swam to the shore that was so close to him, but when I started to swim for it, the shore got farther and farther away."

His dream kind of gave me the creeps, but I could tell that he had been screwed by life a few times too to have a dream like that.

"I'm sorry, Jack, you probably didn't want to hear that," Principal Leonard apologized as he scooted in closer to have his legs under his desk.

"No, it's okay, it was funny," I said, and then, seeing as how I was comfortable with him and he was truly comfortable with me, and not just faking it like most adults, I asked, "Principal Leonard, was Sam ever brought up here? Like, in trouble or anything like that?"

"Hmm…"

He thought about it for a moment, really trying to remember at least one time, but he ended up saying, "No, I don't think so. Sam was a good kid, right?"

"I think he was," I said. "What about other kids coming up and complaining about him?"

"Complaints about Sam?" Principal Leonard asked, questioning this entire conversation. "We're talking about the same Sam, right? Sam Miller?"

"Yes, that Sam," I said, trying not to hint at anything.

"No complaints, more like worship. Sam was a nice guy who wanted to help people. Or at least, that's what I got from when I met him and when other people talked about him. Miss Klein loved having him in class."

"Yeah, we talked about that yesterday," I reinforced.

"Yeah… But no complaints… and I'm not just saying that. Jack, I'm being as straightforward with you as I'd want you to be with me."

Before I could say any more, the final bell of the day rang and Principal Leonard jumped. I was surprised too, but not as much as he was.

"Well, I'll let you go; I'm sure you want to go home now," he said, standing up from his chair.

"Yeah, I guess I will go. But thanks for checking on me, I really do appreciate it."

I walked out of his office and he told me to not mention it, but I was glad I did anyway.

*****

I headed for the parking lot down the main sidewalk after making my way back through the entire school. The buses loaded in the front by the oak tree and the office, and the students parked way in the back by the commons. That made me wonder where the hell the teachers parked.

Anyway, as soon as I started heading to the parking lot, I saw someone standing at my car, and I patted my inner pocket for my knife. (Yes, I took a knife to school. You'd do the same if you were in this situation).

But instead of seeing someone threatening standing by my car, it was Ben. A part of me wished he wasn't there, but maybe we could share information.

Which is exactly what he wanted to do when I walked up to him.

"So…?" Ben asked.

"Nothing much. I crushed the original coping cycle of a loving girlfriend and then almost got caught by the Principal," I said, giving him the crappy report. "You?"

"Oh damn... I haven't really started looking yet... I don't know where to start."

"Well, as long as you don't ask everyone in the damn school I think we'll be fine," I said, a little irked that he didn't look at all.

"So now Emily knows the theory?"

"Yeah, and so does Alyssa," I answered, and when he started giving me a look that said, "You told Alyssa!?" I argued, "It wasn't my choice, Ben, she was right there when I proposed the idea. But she even mentioned helping us."

"So, only four of us know?" Ben asked.

"Yeah, but we don't even 'know' anything anyway, we're just speculating."

"I'm not speculating. I know Sam didn't kill himself."

"You know? So did you kill him?"

"Hell no! Jesus, Jack, why would you even say that?"

"I don't know, just ran out of things to say I guess."

Ben shook his head at me, a little agitated from what I said. But instead of arguing more, he just slowed down and said, "Well, any more ideas since they didn't know anything?"

"No. Honestly, I can't think of anybody who would want to kill Sam. Even if Sam killed a black widow in his backyard or something it wouldn't come back to life to try and kill him and get revenge, it'd come back to life to try and get to know him."

"Well, maybe we should stop trying to think of who would kill him and instead just ask people who were close to Sam?"

"Why do you think I asked Emily?" I asked a little hurt.

"Yeah I know, and I'm not saying that was a bad idea, but how about someone closer... Like... his parents?"

Shocked at what Ben suggested, I gave him the craziest look I could without making it funny and I asked, "What? Are you kidding me, Ben? I'm not going to go to his parents and just say, 'Hey, Mr. and Mrs. Miller, your son didn't commit suicide, but I'm afraid he was murdered.'!"

"Well of course not, that's too grim," Ben said. "No, what you need to do is just bring it on lightly."

"Me? How about us? You come with me."

"No, Jack, I can't. My Dad kills me if I'm home any later than three-ten."

Glancing at my watch, I looked back up at Ben and said, "It's three-fifteen."

Ben's eyes widened like a cheetah seeing the first gazelle of the season and he checked his watch to see if I was just messing with him. When he realized I wasn't just messing with him, he shouted, "Shit! Well, I gotta go, but you should go talk to his parents! Just, don't even say he was murdered, just question the whole situation in general!"

And so, yet again, Ben was leaving me to do the hard stuff all by myself while he satisfied every last wish from his Father.

I would say that Ben owed me, but really, I wanted to do this alone.

Chapter Five
The Talk
The Miller Residence
Tuesday, May 22nd
4 pm

After driving around the Stanton Stretch a little bit to finally gain the courage to talk to Sam's parents, I headed to his house on the south side of town in Stanton Place.

Only a few kids I knew actually lived in Forest Haven. It seemed to be where the new families moved to have the convenience factor of being so close to the school, and then maybe when they decided to move, they'd come on by Stanton Place to see what was for sale.

Recently, I hadn't seen any homes sell in my neighborhood, but the neighborhood was vast and stretched off and around to farther lengths than I wanted to explore, so maybe there was a house somewhere.

But you'd just have to check with a local realtor, today.

Anyway, all jokes aside, when I pulled up to the curb by Sam's house, I got the same sickening feeling I developed when I told Emily the theory about Sam being murdered. This time, I wasn't ready for the sick feeling's return, and I didn't make a warm welcome for it, so it hit me hard and I started to gag like I was about to throw up. Luckily, some bottled water that I had left over from an unknown date was in my cup holder and chugging the rest down helped me not throw up.

For now, that is.

Then, stepping out of my car after putting it in park and turning it off, I felt weird and misplaced while walking up the concrete walkway. The house was inviting with different assorted plants potted on the front porch, but I still had a weird feeling crawling up and down my spine like an indecisive spider.

And even when I stepped up to the door, I choked. Just the thought of talking to Sam's Mom and Dad about the possibility of Sam being killed by another student or just anything other than suicide made me worried about how this would all go down. If Emily flipped, I was sure Sam's parents would too.

But there was no time to stall. I shook off all the weird and sick feelings, opened the glass door, raised my fist up to the wooden door and knocked three times.

To my surprise, I received a quick response.

"Go away; I'm not doing interviews."

"Mrs. Miller?" I called out, recognizing her voice. "It's me, Jack. Jack Sampson."

She didn't even respond, but she didn't have to. Instead, she started unlocking the wooden door and opened it.

"Oh, Jack, dear," she said, coming at me with open arms.

Before I could react, I was tugged into a warm embrace of loss and sorrow, but it felt right.

I patted her back and returned the hug the best I could without letting the glass door hit her on the head. I don't think she'd want to add a concussion to losing her only child.

After what seemed like five minutes, she let go of me and said, "C'mon in, Jack, I thought you were another reporter."

I stepped in behind her and closed the wooden door completely. She walked off toward the kitchen that was just past the living room and I remembered how simple the house was, but it was a nice home.

"Do you want something to drink? I don't have any soda, but I have Cran-Grape juice and purified water?"

I usually just got water from the sink, so I guess I'd try the purified water and see what all the buzz was about.

"Water sounds good," I said.

Last time I was over here with Sam, his Mother offered to get me a drink. When I offered to get it myself, she almost bit my head off. That's why I didn't do it this time.

"With ice?" she asked as she disappeared to search in a cabinet that was out of my line of sight.

As I stepped into the living room a little more, I answered, "Maybe a cube or two."

In a few seconds, she came back out, water glass in a hand with a cube or two surfacing at the top. Handing it to me when it was almost about to overflow, I sucked the top to try and deplete the supply a little before spilling it everywhere.

"Oh, don't stand like you've never been here before. Sit down on the loveseat!"

I did what she said, trying to make it seem like I was just coming by for a little visit. Maybe if I chickened out, I'd turn it into that.

"How was school, Jack?" Mrs. Miller asked before sitting down on the couch across from me.

A coffee table divided us and I felt a little safer since she wasn't in the radius of being able to grab my neck and choke me to death when I ran the theory by her.

Throwing the crazy ideas out, I answered, "It was pretty good, I–"

"Actually, Jack, if you don't mind me saying," she started, not even noticing she cut me off, "I thought you were Sam at first when you pulled up... but then I knew I was just being too hopeful for no reason and that you were probably just another reporter."

She was having the same problem I was, thinking that Sam would just walk back into our lives one day and say it was his one big joke to us for all the jokes we did to him, but that wasn't the case, and we both knew it.

So, instead of dreading on that topic, I asked, "Are reporters bothering you a lot?"

"Well, mainly last week, and they did come by yesterday just to try for the last time, but they haven't been by today, thank God."

"That's good," I said, not really understanding why the reporters would be so interested anyway. The only time one came out here was when Manny Dulog broke the record for eating the most hot dogs at some contest up in Flint.

"Is Sam's car still here?" I followed up asking, just out of curiosity.

"Oh, yeah, it's in the garage," Mrs. Miller said. "We're thinking about selling it to our nephew in Kansas. Would you like to go see it?"

"No, I don't think I'm ready for something like that," I honestly said.

Mrs. Miller nodded lightly.

"You miss him a lot, don't you?"

Not really expecting the question, I replied, "Well, yes, of course. Both Emily and I are taking it hard, but I know you and–"

"What about the other kids at school? Like... Gregory Allen? They were good friends at one point," Mrs. Miller asked.

For some reason, I wanted to tell her how kids at school didn't seem to care anymore and just be upfront about the entire thing, but I held back and said, "Yeah, we talk about him every day."

Mrs. Miller exhaled sadly and I took a cold drink of water.

"You kids shouldn't have to go through something like that. I don't know why Sam did it, but he must've had a pretty good reason. Like any parent, I blamed myself at first…"

"No, you shouldn't blame yourself," I said. "You and your husband are great parents, and Sam was really a reflection of the two of you put together. When my dad was killed, I actually looked up to you and your husband for guidance, but Sam always knew what you guys would say to my problems."

Mrs. Miller smiled, and said on a lighter note, "I hope Sam didn't tell you to break up with that sweet girl, Alyssa? Because I wouldn't have said to do that."

"No, he didn't… that was all me," I admitted.

"What a shame," Mrs. Miller said. "Well, you're a nice kid, she'll take you back."

"Ha-ha," I said, not really in the mood to talk about my love life to Sam's Mom.

After my laugh, I heard another door in the house open and close pretty quickly and Mrs. Miller looked over her shoulder while calling out, "Honey, is that you?"

"Yup, I'm home," Mr. Miller said, sounding tired and beat.

"Jack came by to visit," Mrs. Miller informed.

Mr. Miller stuck his head out from the kitchen and said, "Oh, hey, Jack. Hope things are going well."

"As good as they can be," I returned.

Mr. Miller nodded, understanding exactly what I meant, and he walked past us to go to the staircase by the front door, undoing his plaid tie as he walked.

When Mrs. Miller and I were alone again, I had a feeling that now was the time to ask about Sam's possible killing.

Starting softly, I asked, "Mrs. Miller, earlier you said you didn't know why Sam killed himself."

"That's right," Mrs. Miller answered softly, and after clearing her throat, she spoke up to add, "It really beats me. Everyone liked Sam and Sam liked everyone else."

"I know he did," I replied, and then, taking a dive, I tried out bringing on the theory. "None of this makes sense to me either, or to Emily or Ben

Whey… So… it kinda makes you wonder if maybe it wasn't suicide…"

Mrs. Miller raised an eyebrow at me and squinted her eyes in a confused way.

"What?"

"Well, you agree with me, don't you? Suicide just seems completely ridiculous, so I thought—"

"You're saying someone killed my boy? My sweet, loving boy?"

"That's what I think," I said, coming clean.

But just like with Emily, the thought of murder made everything ten times worse and she began crying almost immediately. I felt bad for bringing it up, but I had to find out.

"I'm sorry Mrs. Miller, but I just want to know if you can think of anyone who could've done it… Someone in my grade?"

Her eyes opened with the tears still rushing out, and just as I thought she had something to say, she looked up at me and I knew what was going on.

"What the hell!?"

Mr. Miller yelled out and walked over to us at the end of the coffee table. Mrs. Miller continued crying harder while his eyes stabbed into me. My heart skipped a few beats and I feared what would happen.

"You little bastard, get the hell out of my house and take your stupid teenage drama with you!"

I didn't want to argue with him, but what he said really hurt me and I tried to show him that with the look on my face. He just pointed toward the door and raised his other hand at me, almost like he was going to drag me out of the house.

Before he could, I stood up and let myself out, and he locked the door behind me.

I felt like I was probably not welcome to their house anymore.

Great idea, Ben…

But I couldn't just blame him. Maybe if I would've stood up and said something to Mr. Miller too, he would've understood what I was trying to say. But now, I had to leave as I headed for my car, hoping that I could just go home and forget about everything.

Making two women cry on the same day really made me wonder if I was a good person or not.

*****

With nothing else to do or pursue, I decided to just call it a day and go on home. Driving down the cool streets with my windows down helped me start to relax and feel better about myself, although I still regretted going to the Miller's house. It just seemed wrong. The last thing Sam's parents wanted to hear was that their son was murdered. It was the last thing I wanted to hear too, but that's not how it worked out. Now, it was just a game of Battleship, with random guessing that only eased your mind once you hit the other person's ship.

Forgetting how close Sam's house was to mine, I quickly pulled into my driveway, wishing I could just drive around a little longer, but I decided to go on inside since I was already there. After closing my door and locking my car, I unlocked my front door and stepped into the living room to sit on the couch and stare at our Toshiba flat screen TV without even turning it on. I knew what was on TV without even turning it on though: Stupid sitcoms, reruns of old TV shows from when my mom was younger, and cartoons that made the ones I watched when I was a kid look twenty times better.

Nothing seemed to be going right.

Checking my phone, I saw I didn't have any text messages whatsoever. To me, it was peaceful, but to other teenagers, they'd start texting people in desperation. I thought about calling Emily, but maybe she just wanted to be alone. And I thought about texting Ben, but I just wanted to be alone.

As I sat around on the couch, out of curiosity, I wondered where the remote was. It wasn't on either armrest or the marble table in front of me. I then wondered when the last time was that anyone watched TV in the living room, and I felt spoiled for having such a big TV that I didn't even use.

So, in the quest for the TV remote, I stood up and walked around the room, wondering if maybe it was under the table or the couch. When that didn't work out, I headed for the TV itself and found the remote sitting by the DVR. Both had about the same amount of dust on them, and I laughed. What a waste...

But then, right before I walked off, I saw my Xbox 360 sitting on its side with a few games to the left of it. The first one I saw brought me back, back to a memory of my dad that sort of applied now more than ever.

Back in seventh grade, my Dad had been home for a few days since his second deployment, so I wasn't always running up to him and hugging him at that point. Instead, I kicked back and started playing Call of Duty as my mom dusted around the house and my Dad ran to the grocery store for a few things. Prior to playing the game, my Mom had me not play it for a few days after my Dad got home because she said it might upset him, but after begging and pleading, I got what I wanted and I was able to shoot some Nazis.

I was having fun and kicking digital ass, but it ended pretty soon.

My Dad walked in the front door, his hands were full of bags and he sounded a little out of breath. He met my Mom halfway in the living room and as she took some of the bags, he kissed her.

Just as they kissed, a bomb went off in the game and my Dad looked over at it.

"What's that? Something on TV?" my Dad asked, not sounding too mad yet.

"No, it's just this little game that Jack is playing," my Mom said, trying to be on my side.

But it didn't work for very long at all. My Dad stepped away from my Mom and his anger got the best of him like it sometimes did.

"A game? War's not a game, Amanda," my Dad scolded.

That's when I actually tuned into the conversation completely and turned away from the TV screen. When my Dad called my Mom by her first name, I knew something was wrong.

"Jack, I want you to turn that game off and go to your room, do you understand me!?" my dad shouted.

The wimpy child version of me appeared in my memory and I replied, "Yes, Dad!"

I was scared… so scared I ran out of the room and didn't even turn the game off or pause it.

I went up to my room and started crying instead. I felt like some kind of failure of a son, never making Dad proud when he came back from his deployment. Instead, I was some little punk who thought it was fun to kill a bunch of people. When I was a kid, it was just a game… I didn't understand why my Dad really didn't like it until he died.

That night, right before dinner, my Dad walked into my room very quietly and non-threatening. I buried my face into my pillow, scared of what was going to happen, but all the fear went away when I heard my Dad speak softly to me.

"Jack, mind if I sit by you?"

I shook my head no and he sat at the edge of my bed, his right hand reached over and patted me on the back lightly.

"I'm sorry," I said, trying to get back on his good side.

"No, son, I'm sorry," my Dad said. "It's just… I mean, you're getting older, so I want to explain something to you, but I want you to look at me when I do. It has a better effect that way."

I turned around in my bed to have my back against the mattress and my eyes gleaming up at my Dad with a few dried tears on my face.

He felt bad as he wiped the tears away and he said, "Listen to me, Jack, and listen closely. I want you… Well, I just want to make sure you don't think death and violence and war is a game, I mean, do you? Because I understand in those games, it can actually be fun to pull the trigger and blast away the enemy troops… But in real life, it's not fun. It's truly a matter of life and death. Those people on that game want to kill you, but once you're killed, you can come right back to life and everything is fine. But out there on the battlefield… Well, I don't want to tell you too much, and you shouldn't worry about me when I'm over there because I'm careful. But I've taken a man's life before, and it's not like that game portrays it. Death is a serious thing, and I just wanted to make sure you understand that it's not just a game.

"I… got upset because a bomb went off pretty close to us a few months ago and took down an entire building, and I felt like I was just inches away. I've lost friends over there, and I try to move on, but I can't. And the more people I shoot over there, the emptier I feel on the inside. Even if my captain tries to convince me that killing those bastards over there will bring my fallen friends closer to redemption, I still feel empty. So once I get home, and I see that my son is doing the same thing I had to do, it just got the best of me, and I'm sorry. I know in that instance it's just a game, but for me, it's life."

At the time he told me all of that, it didn't really sink in and change my life forever or anything like that. I just listened and accepted his apology. But now, I knew what my Dad meant, and I felt the same way. What would finding Sam's killer really even prove? Nothing. It wouldn't bring Sam back, or make me feel like I did something great. It was just… Whatever. I cared about Sam and I still do, but maybe looking for his killer was just for my sake. I was doing it for myself, not for everyone else…

"Jack, I'm home."

My Mom came in through the garage and closed the door behind her. I stood up and left the memory and remote behind by the TV.

My Mom looked in from the kitchen to the side and asked, "I'm about to make dinner. Did you drop something?"

"No, I didn't lose anything," I replied. "Why are you home so early?"

My Mom gave me a weird look and said, "What are you talking about? It's six-fifty, just like usual."

I looked at my watch and she was right. Jesus Christ, I got home at five o'clock and that memory... must've gone by really slow. Maybe I played it in my head more than once and I just didn't remember now...

Just like in the shower when I spent too long, or when I brushed my teeth forever. What was wrong with me?

I felt like I was having more repercussions from this whole mess than anyone else was, but that thought seemed conceited.

"Are you okay, Jack?"

My Mom's concerned tone of voice made me feel loved once more by someone and I answered, "Yeah, Mom, I'm good. How was work?"

"Ugh, the usual. I got yelled at for losing the supreme court briefs, even though Stacy just 'misplaced' it."

My Mom always mentioned people from her work, but I never remembered who any of them were. To me, it was a bunch of faceless names.

"But you got it back, right?"

"Well of course, once I pulled it out from under Stacy's fat ass. She actually got mad at me for even saying she was the last one to have it, but I proved it to her that she had it. Now, who do you think should get yelled at?"

"I'm thinking Stacy," I guessed confidently.

"Yeah, but guess what? Not a word was said to her."

Same thing would happen at school on a daily basis. Not anytime recently, but all of the rest of the time. But, I didn't tell my Mom about each time it happened, mainly because a million dollars wasn't at stake.

"So, what do you want for dinner?" my Mom asked, changing the subject after a long sigh. "Lasagna or... lasagna?"

"With choices like that, I'm going to have to go with lasagna," I replied with a small smile.

"Wanna help me with it?" she asked.

"Uh, sure."

*****

At about 7:45, we were finally eating dinner at the table for the first time in a while, and I wondered when the last time was that we both sat down and ate together. Seemed like a lot of firsts were happening today... but none of them were really that exciting.

I tried to take a bite of the lasagna, but it was too hot and I really wasn't in the mood to burn my tongue. I thought about things I was in the mood for, but a few weren't appropriate.

"So, Jack, how's school?" my Mom asked.

"It's going," I answered.

"Well, is that good or bad?"

"A little of both."

"Well, then that's good. Nothing hurts when there's a little equality."

"Yeah, I guess so," I said darkly.

My Mom caught onto my tone and gave me a funny look.

"Now wait just a minute, Jack, what happened to the little of both? Now you just make everything seem worse."

"I miss Sam, Mom, that's all."

My Mom scrunched her face and said, "I know sweetie, it's really hard when a friend passes."

"Didn't someone die when you were in high school?"

My Mom wiped some lasagna sauce off of her face and said, "So, I guess we're going to surf the morbid topics at tonight's dinner, are we?"

I shook my head at her joke and replied, "I just want to be able to relate."

My Mom squeezed my arm with her thumb on my elbow and her index finger on the inner side.

"Okay honey, yes, a classmate of mine died senior year. But out where I lived, this was common. You know, back in Illinois at a big six-A school. Kids died every year, almost like a tradition. It was sad, but most of the time, I didn't know the kids that well."

"What do you mean?"

"Well, you know how the younger classes are really big at your school? Like... the four hundred ninth graders or whatever? That's how many seniors we had in my class, and by the time senior year rolled around, sure, we all knew each other, but we just had certain groups of people that we stayed close to, not really everyone mashed together as one big group with different sections like at your school."

"Why did we move out here then?" I asked, never remembering asking before.

"Your father wanted to, but I'm not sure why exactly. He once said his grandpa used to live out here and he loved coming here during the summer. Also, your father wasn't too crazy about his family, so we shipped out over here all by ourselves."

"Oh, okay," I said, not really too convinced on the idea. "But, how did the person die?"

"Car wreck, after a graduation party," my Mom said, taking another bite of lasagna. "Yeah… It was her and a few guys all packed in a car and driving around, probably fishtailing the entire way to… wherever they were going. Surprisingly, as drunk as they were they wore seatbelts, but that didn't help them in this situation. Y'see, right outside of the city I grew up in as you headed south, there was this big lake that seemed like it should've been classified with the rest of the Great Lakes. Anyway, the road curved as you drove along it, but the driver didn't realize that, so he just drove straight and busted through the almost meaningless barrier going about eighty miles per hour, and they landed pretty far into the lake so they couldn't swim back. The police said they drowned since they were too drunk to even know how to unbuckle their seatbelts."

"Wow, that's pretty messed up," I commented.

"Yeah, well I actually turned in the parents who had the party."

"What?"

"You heard me, parents, supplying a bunch of dumb graduates with liquor and not even taking their keys away. I heard about the party, I just didn't want to go. I knew something was going to happen. And once I found out the girl in the car was Lisa, I told the police I knew where the party was held and who was responsible for the drinking in the first place. Poor Lisa Hannigan, died in a car with three guys; who I heard she had slept with them before, but I don't know that for sure."

I spit up a little of my water out of shock from what my Mom said.

"What? Not like it's the first time you've heard about that kind of stuff," my mom said. "Or maybe it is… which is why a small town is helpful. And God is this small town close-knit. But at the same time, that's why it hurts so badly when something terrible finally happens. You have no experience on the matter."

"Yeah, we really don't," I agreed.

"But I turned in those parents, and swore to myself I'd never let my kid ever do something like that. They got arrested pretty soon afterward, and a few kids actually complained that I turned them in! They said there wasn't a place to party anymore, but I was doing them all a favor."

I was close to finishing my lasagna but my Mom called for my attention again.

"Jack, I don't want you doing anything like that the night after graduation, you hear me? Do the right thing. Go to the graduation thingy the school keeps sending home ads for. Because even if there are parents at a party you go to, that just isn't cool."

I nodded with a laugh coming over me finally, and she laughed with me, knowing that I wouldn't do anything like that.

But just before I was done, I looked at my Mom and realized she had done the same thing when she was my age. She did what was right, and told the police where that party happened. I didn't care if finding Sam's killer wouldn't bring Sam back, it was all about bringing justice to Sam so he wasn't thought of in a negative way for killing himself, but rather a more positive way for staring death in the face... Literally.

I finished with my lasagna with new hopes and I thanked my Mom for the meal, which then led to me going back up to my room and closing the door behind me.

My cell phone was out before the door even closed completely and I dialed up Ben.

"Hello?"

"Hi, I guess you're not dead," I started.

"Hah," Ben replied. "Almost. I had to bribe my little sister to not tell on me this time. She doesn't really understand what's going on... Anyway, what's up?"

"I talked to the Millers, but mainly Sam's Mom."

"Oh yeah? And?"

"She didn't say anything. She ended up crying and I was thrown out of their house by Sam's Dad, who didn't seem very happy. If I remember right, I think he said something along the lines of, 'You little bastard, get the hell out of my house, and take your stupid teenage drama with you!' It was pretty fun."

"Oh, I'm sorry, Jack," Ben said. "I guess maybe we're just a little too hopeful."

"No, I still believe that Sam was killed. There's just no way it was suicide."

"But, Jack, all we're doing is upsetting people."

"No, I'm upsetting people. You're just sitting behind the protective barrier hearing it all from me."

"Hey, I'm on your side you know," Ben argued.

I started to calm down and so I replied, "Yeah, I do know, sorry."

"It's okay. What about Sam's parents?"

"What about them?"

"Would they…"

"Oh, don't even suggest that!" I urged.

"Jack, just think for a second. They went out that night on a date, and it was a Monday. What parents go out on a date on a Monday?"

"Ben, just listen to me. Sam's parents are both great people who are just going through a hard time, like you and me and Emily. There's no way they killed Sam, trust me."

"Keep an open mind," Ben said, not backing away from his theory.

"Maybe it was their anniversary! I don't know," I tried to argue.

"That's still weird."

"But even if it was their anniversary, Sam wouldn't have planned it then. He would've waited for another day, to not ruin their night."

"When would it not ruin their night, Jack?"

He was right. Sam killing himself would've ruined their night any night.

"And besides, it sounds like you're saying it's suicide again. If it was murder, the other person planned it, not Sam."

"So… A potential stalker, who knew that his parents were leaving that night?" I asked.

"It's completely possible. In a small town like this, people always complain that there's nothing to do."

"Yeah, stalking Sam is what I used to do in my free time," I said sarcastically, and then, thinking of something, "Did Sam ever have a really nasty breakup? I don't recall any."

"What… a psycho ex-girlfriend?"

"Sure, why not. Seems like the other theories aren't really working," I said.

"Maybe," Ben replied, and I heard some foreign chatter in the background. "Look, Jack, I have to go. See you at school, if I can find you during the practice graduation."

I had forgotten about that. Tomorrow, we were going to take a bus to The First Baptist Church in another city a few miles away to practice walking around and grabbing our diplomas. I wasn't excited for it at all.

"Yeah, take it easy," I said to Ben, and then hung up the phone.

After plugging my phone into the charger, and realizing I didn't care what was being spread on Facebook, I lay down on my bed and started thinking about what all was going on until I fell asleep.

Senior year… I had completely forgotten about the practice graduation, or even graduating at all. A part of me wasn't so thrilled after all the stuff with Sam happened, but I should cheer up just a little bit to where I'm not such a jerk. People around me seemed a little repulsed by my attitude, so I guess I'd have to lighten up a little bit until I graduate, or until I find who killed Sam.

Speaking of that, now Ben and I were going off the idea that it was either Sam's parents or a psycho ex-girlfriend. But honestly, the only girl Sam ever dated that ended badly was Jessica Pivlett: A girl who most people dated even though she had a last name which sounded almost like piglet. But then the ridicule stopped once she developed earlier than all the other girls and developed until the day she moved away toward the end of eighth grade. I think that was one of Sam's only other mistakes. He just dated her because he was popular and she was popular, and that was it. No other reason. They never met each other's parents, never really went out anywhere: it was just a school relationship that ended in relation-shit.

But, she moved all the way to Maine. Would she really come back four years later just to settle a score that never existed? I remember the day they broke up. Sam walked up to her at lunch and told her how it was, and she got mad, to say the least.

But besides her, I really couldn't think of anyone else who would've been a psycho ex-girlfriend of Sam's. Except…

Well, ever since the funeral… when Emily held my hand… I thought that was okay, but then she did again in Government…

No, why would I even think that she could be Sam's killer? Now I'm just desperate to find someone.

That's when I decided to go on to sleep and dream it all out. Maybe some dream would give me the answer.

But then I remembered that I can't dream. Not yet, anyway.

CHAPTER SIX
THE STIR
FIRST BAPTIST CHURCH
WEDNESDAY, MAY 23RD
8:30 AM

The seniors of Stanton High School took two buses to The First Baptist Church in some big city that I didn't even care to know the name of. When I walked on over to the buses, I couldn't find Ben anywhere, so I went on the first bus, thinking he might be on it, but he wasn't. Instead, I ended up sitting by Harold, Mark, and Nick, who all seemed glad that I stopped by.

"Hi again, Jack," Nick greeted me.

Alyssa wasn't on this bus either, or Emily, so I guess I picked the "loser" bus, but I could care less.

"Hi, fellas," I said, trying to be a bit more jovial. "Harold, can you move your backpack? What do you need that for anyway?"

"I just… you never know! What if they pull out some final assignment that we were never warned about and you have to take it no matter what, prepared or not! Well, I'm prepared," Harold said confidently.

"That's great, Harold, really great," I answered.

Nick and Mark shared a laugh at Harold's expense and Harold looked bothered at me, but that's when I said, "Oh c'mon Harold, I'm only teasing."

"Well, he wasn't!" Mark almost shouted. "Harold actually thinks there will be some random final assignment from the teachers, and he'll be the only student with a pencil and some paper."

"I heard it from my cousin in Florida!" Harold finally explained. "Right before she graduated, the last day of school, her last hour teacher gave out a survey about the whole high school experience and she didn't have a single thing on her! Dropped her from an A to a B!"

"Hey, isn't that your cousin who I met? Who gets nervous way too easily?" Nick asked.

"Yeah, she threw up all over the survey when she couldn't find a pen," Harold said sadly.

Just as I started laughing with the rest of them, a teacher at the front of the bus who I didn't know started checking who was and wasn't on this bus. I guess it would've worked better if they would've just done alphabetical order, but whatever. That's why I didn't work at the school.

Once the teacher stopped talking, Nick and Mark turned back around to look at Harold and me so Nick could begin a new conversation.

"So, I was playing that game last night, you know, the Grave Robber one that Mark asked you about the other day, Jack, and just as I was pickpocketing some old dude in this run-down town that I hadn't even finished exploring yet, some random weird glitch happened and the friggin' sun fell on me!"

"Oh quiet down, Nick," Harold complained. "I don't want to hear about that game, it's so boring."

"Boring!? I'll tell you what's boring: A generic FPS with nothing new to offer, but they come out every year!"

"I haven't even played any FPS's in a long time!" Harold argued. "I actually went back in time and plugged in my older brother's NES. Now that's some fun stuff."

"So what, you're AVGN now?" Mark asked.

"No, I just enjoy the classics," Harold explained. And right when Nick started to interject, Harold finished, "And I don't use emulators."

Nick backed off in defeat and I laughed at how nerdy their conversation was, or maybe I laughed because I understood everything they were talking about.

Finally, the teacher up at the front said we were ready to go and we pulled away from the school, heading for the big city.

On the way to the church about halfway there, Harold eventually gained the courage to ask me a question that was bugging him.

"Hey, Jack, if you don't mind me asking," he started, and I stopped playing BrickBreaker on my phone to listen to him, "what happened with Emily yesterday?"

"How did you hear about it?" I asked, starting to worry.

"She came into seventh hour late, talking about how you upset her at lunch, but she said she knew you didn't mean to… How did you upset her?" Harold asked.

"Oh, she didn't tell you?"

Harold shook his head and I saw Nick and Mark start to gain interest in the conversation.

"Well, that's good."

"I was wondering if you could tell me what happened," Harold asked again.

"Why do you want to know?"

"Well," Nick said, and he turned around while adjusting his glasses, "now Harold isn't the only one who wants to know."

"Dammit," I said under my breath. "Look it's hard to explain and you'll probably just laugh at me."

"Us laugh at you?" Mark asked. "When Harold first said he was friends with you, we were skeptical to the max. There was no way Harold could have a friend as cool as you."

"I'm cool?" I asked.

"Oh c'mon, don't act like you don't know," Nick said. "You have the bad boy look that every girl loves, somehow combined with the nice guy personality that everyone loves and appreciates."

"Yeah, and when you beat Raymond Todd to a pulp," Mark said, "you were kind of my hero after that."

I looked at Harold to see if he was laughing, knowing they were joking, but his face was straight as an arrow as I asked, "Really?"

"They're being serious, Jack. I even had a girl approach me for the first and last time ever asking me for your number," Harold explained.

I knew which girl he was talking about, but it didn't matter now.

"Well," I said, and never really picked up from it. The truth was, I knew I was popular, but not that I was considered cool... When did this happen?

"So, can you tell us?" Mark asked.

"Eh," I said, glancing around the bus and then lowering my voice, "how about when we're coming back to the school? Seems like more than just the four of us are listening in right now."

I saw a few eyes turn away, now knowing that I wasn't giving in that easily, and the "fellas" seemed to understand why I didn't say it yet. But the more I thought about it, the more I didn't want to.

*****

When we got to the church, we piled in to start the fake graduation and see what it'd be like without the crazily high emotions. I was surprised to see Emily and Alyssa going to sit somewhere way at the front of the church to hear Principal Leonard's instructions. Right before they sat down, I guess they felt me staring at them, because they both turned around and didn't

83

seem too surprised to see me. Luckily, to show we were still friends, Emily waved at me lightly and I returned one to her. But Alyssa just sort of smiled at me halfway and I tried to return one back, but right when I did, someone grabbed my shoulder and I turned around.

"Jack," Ben said, seeming out of breath. "I've been looking for you and texting you forever! Where have you been?"

"I took the first bus because I couldn't find you," I answered.

"Oh, I took the second bus because they said the first bus was full."

"Well, I'm sorry."

"Don't be," Ben said, and then he brought up the conversation that I really didn't feel like having. "Did you think of anyone last night?"

"I don't think this is the time or place, but since we both know what we're talking about, I'll just be vague," I said critically, and then continued. "Yes, but the only possible psycho ex I could think of was Jessica."

"Jessica…" Ben said, trying to remember her.

"You know, Jessica Pivlett? Eighth grade?"

"Oh yeah, Piglet," Ben said with a laugh. "But she's all the way in Maine now, so she wouldn't have done it."

"Yeah, I thought of that too. And honestly, that was the only girl I could think of."

"You did better than me at least. I couldn't think of a single one."

Harold walked up to me with Nick and Mark and our conversation began to fold.

"Hey, Ben, how's it going?" Harold asked.

"It's uh; it's going pretty good, thanks. How about you?"

"Can't complain, just glad we don't have to wear those ghastly robes yet," Harold answered.

"Oh, yeah, well, we can talk later, Jack," Ben said.

"Yeah, I agree. I'll call you if something comes up."

Ben walked off and Harold looked at me, a little aggravated.

"What?" I said.

"So the Asian can know, but not us?"

"Don't call him 'the Asian'. Besides, he's the one that made the idea that I'll share with you later."

"Oh, well okay then," Harold said.

"Yeah Harold, calm down," Nick said, and when I saw him adjusting his glasses, I couldn't even guess what joke he was going to make. "We're really dealing with two OG's up in here, we better step off."

"What are OG's?" Harold asked.

I groaned and Mark did too.

"OG: Original Gangster; the founders?"

I laughed because Harold looked completely dumbfounded, but he tried to save himself by saying, "Oh, yeah, I knew that."

*****

For some reason, and I've never been able to figure out why the damn thing lasted all day long. At one point, I wondered just exactly how far this place was from my small town because it had to be the drive there and the drive back to school that took the most time, because otherwise...

Well, there were a few times where people wouldn't get into alphabetical order because they wanted to stand by their friends. I ended up standing next to someone I hadn't talked to probably since kindergarten. His name was Max Silberstein, and I remembered having trouble with his last name back then, but now I could say it correctly because my IQ was a little higher.

We talked, he apologized about Sam, I asked if they were close, he said no, and that was about it. But we had to stand by each other the entire day, which wasn't too bad. He was pretty funny, and he kept making jokes about other people and how some weird guy was staring at us while we practiced.

It made me laugh, and I felt like today was the first good day since everything had happened. Maybe Principal Leonard's talk, combined with the memory of my dad and my conversation with my mom really helped out a lot. Now I was able to enjoy the day a little more, while still missing Sam on the side, instead of missing Sam being the main part of my day.

On the bus ride home, I sat by the same "fellas" I did on the way to the church. They were lively and fun, but then, of course, Harold had to ask once again why Emily was so upset.

"Do you really want to know?" I asked.

"Yes, why else would I be asking?" Harold countered.

"Fine," I gave in. Mark and Nick turned around to listen and I made sure no one else was. Everyone else just listened to iPods or MP3s or had their own conversations going, so I said, "Well, how do I start this... Sam's suicide surprised you guys, didn't it?"

"I'm pretty sure it surprised everyone," Harold said.

Nick and Mark nodded in agreement and I continued.

"Okay, well it surprised me too, and Ben Whey. So Monday, after school, he suggested an idea."

"C'mon, tell us," Nick pleaded.

Cringing at the thought of what has happened every other time I've shared the theory, I let them have it.

"What if I said that Sam didn't commit suicide, but he was murdered?"

Surprisingly enough, Nick, Mark, and Harold all leaned back and just thought about it for a second instead of flipping out and calling me a bastard.

When one of them thought of something to say, Harold replied, "I think that makes sense."

"Really? You do?" I asked.

Mark nodded.

"It makes more sense than suicide. I never really met Sam, except at the bowling alley, but he didn't seem like the kind of guy who'd do that."

"I agree completely," Nick said.

"Well, this is the best reaction I've gotten from telling anyone about it," I started to say. "But don't tell anyone about this. Ben and I think it might be someone in our grade."

"Really? But who would kill Sam?" Harold asked.

"What if it was an ex-girlfriend?" Mark asked.

"Yeah, already thought about that. The only ex of Sam's that would even just think about doing that, in my opinion, is Jessica Pivlett."

A perv-ish smile ran across Nick's face and I was tempted to smack it off, but then I'd be a hypocrite.

"Well maybe," Mark said, "it was one of Sam's friends who was jealous of his popularity. I mean… Gregory Allen wanted to be the quarterback just as much as Sam, maybe even more."

"You follow sports?" Nick asked.

"Look, that's not the point," I said. "Mark, I like that idea."

But I hated the thought: that Gregory Allen might've killed Sam just to have the last word, the last win, the last hoo-ha. But still, not even having proof that Gregory did it, I wanted to sock him in the face.

Mark was happy that I agreed with him, and I was glad that more people were on my side, so I ran by other ideas.

"What do you think about the parents doing it?" I asked.

"No, no, no, no," Harold said.

Mark elaborated as if they could read each other's minds.

"I talked to Sam's parents for a little bit at the bowling alley and they seemed like nice people."

"But besides that," Nick said, adjusting his glasses in an intelligent way for the first time, "Sam's parents have a perfect alibi for the night. There's no way they could've done it. The cops said the time of death was ten minutes before the Millers even got home."

"Yeah, you're right, Nick," I said, surprised that I actually agreed with him on something.

"So that's what made Emily upset?" Harold asked. "You ran the idea by her and she didn't like it?"

"Basically," I answered. "But I don't blame her. When Ben said it to me, I got a little upset, but not that bad. And, I talked to Sam's Mom about it yesterday but I got thrown out by Sam's Dad for making her cry."

"So who all knows then?" Nick asked.

"What about the police?" Mark followed up.

"I talked to the police right after talking to Ben but they don't want to help."

"I see why," Harold said. "Jesus, whoever did this knew what they were doing to make it look like a suicide."

"Yeah, which is a scary thought if it's someone in our grade," I commented. "And I'm the one looking for him."

"Detective Sampson, eh?" Mark asked.

"Please don't call me that," I said.

"Hey! I asked you a question," Nick said, sounding irritated.

"Oh, yeah, sorry Nick. Who all knows, right? Well, now it's the police, the Millers, you, me, Harold, Mark, Ben, Emily, and Alyssa."

"Oh! Alyssa," Nick said seductively.

"Yeah… That wasn't my choice," I tried to defend myself.

"Don't worry, Jack," Nick said and started adjusting his glasses. I was just glad the spitting had stopped. "The good guy always gets the girl in the end."

"That's not why I ran it by her… She sticks to Emily like glue."

"Well, wouldn't you? She lost her boyfriend," Harold sympathized.

"Or are you just wishing Alyssa stuck to you?" Nick asked.

"Nick, I swear, you are barking up the wrong tree right now," I warned.

We all went quiet for a second, and I felt bad for getting upset, but Nick should've known that it was getting annoying by now. But why did it bother me so much? Maybe I did want Alyssa to stick to me like glue, but in our last relationship we just used tape; it still hurt when we separated, but pulling it off was too easy.

*****

At school, we all waited outside by the oak tree like we were told to because the final bell of the day was going to ring soon. I met up with Ben to tell him about running it by Harold, Mark, and Nick.

"Wait, what!?" Ben started, not sounding very happy at all. "You told three people at the same time?"

"I meant to only tell Harold, but the other two stooges listened in too," I replied. "But look, I don't regret it. They actually had a lot of really good input about the whole situation and they gave us another lead."

"Seriously?" Ben asked, about as shocked as I was. "Who?"

"Gregory Allen. They said he really wanted to be the quarterback this year, but Sam got it instead."

"That's a good hunch... How about I talk to him since you've talked to everyone else, eh?"

"I thought you'd never ask," I replied.

Just as the conversation ceased, Alyssa came up behind Ben and started to squeeze her way into our line. A little nervous looking, she batted her eyes at me and said, "Jack, uh, sorry if I'm interrupting, but I wanted to ask if you wanted to—"

Suddenly, she was cut off by another voice that was behind me and I shuddered.

"Mr. Sampson!"

It was a familiar voice, and when I turned around, I saw Detective Donovan in a police cruiser with some other driver I didn't know, but he was another police officer. A few kids around us started "oohing" and I wondered why they were here.

"Come on in the car with us, we need to talk," Donovan said.

I turned back around to face Alyssa and I said, "I'm sorry, I guess I have to go."

"I'll be by your car when you get back," she said, and I knew she was telling the truth.

Everyone's eyes were on me, just like they had been on Monday, and I turned back around to start walking toward the police car. Donovan pointed to the back of the cruiser and I got in the backseat with my heart pumping hard enough to power this city.

Either they had good news for me or really bad news.

*****

When we got to the police station, Donovan actually grabbed at my shirt collar and made sure that I was following him. I struggled and tried to tell him to let go, but he said "No", and we made our way to Chief Ramzorin's office. That's when I knew how serious this was and it was definitely bad news.

Donovan closed the door behind us and Chief Ramzorin stared at me with everlasting sorrow in his eyes. Now I knew I did something wrong and I had a feeling I knew what it was.

"Jack, I'm not going to bullshit with you, so I'll just get right to the point," Chief Ramzorin started in a meaner tone than I had ever heard from him. "I got a call from Mr. Miller yesterday, saying you stopped by their house. Do you want to explain yourself right now or do you want me to go ahead and tell you what I know?"

My grim mood from earlier this week made its second debut by asking, "How about you tell me what you know since I have no idea what that might be?"

"Don't lie to us!" Donovan scolded.

"Donovan, stand down," Chief Ramzorin ordered.

Surprised by the outburst, Donovan backed off and I waited for Chief Ramzorin's response. All of us knew what was going on.

"Jack, Mr. Miller said that when he talked to his wife about why she got upset when you were over there, she said that you said Sam was murdered. Is that true?"

"I think it's true that Sam was murdered," I said slyly.

"You show respect to the Chief!" Donovan shouted and I turned my head away from his annoying voice.

"Donovan, I said shut up!" Chief Ramzorin shouted, which surprised both of us and I was glad my bladder wasn't full, otherwise...

"Chief, I'm sorry if I disrespected you," I said, "but I just don't think you understand how crazy the concept is of someone like Sam killing himself."

"I think it's even crazier that I have some senior in high school in my town who should be worried about his future but instead wants to investigate some fabricated lead by himself about his best friend being murdered."

"I'm the detective in this town, not you," Donovan said.

Chief Ramzorin glared at Donovan and commanded, "Get out of my office, now."

Donovan sneered at me one last time and then left the office, closing the door behind him and having the wood blinds bounce off the glass. Chief Ramzorin then looked back at me and said, "Jack, I don't know why you can't realize that your friend killed himself for some... okay, I do get it. But trust me, son, it's suicide, not murder. If you were at the scene... goddammit, there was so much blood it reminded me of... Never mind. The point is; you really upset the Millers even more than they already were, and I know you're upset too, but just try to cope with the idea that Sam killed himself. I don't know why, you don't know why, nobody knows why, but you just have to live with the fact that it was suicide. It's hard, I know, it's very hard."

"Then why give me your card at the funeral and tell me to call you if something comes up. What exactly is the 'something'?" I argued, on the verge of crying from thinking about Sam's dead body.

"If you were feeling down and wanted to talk to someone other than your mother. I know how that was, always having to talk to your mother because there wasn't a father around. It gets tiring after a while, doesn't it?"

"Chief Ramzorin, I know you say it was suicide, but trust me, it wasn't!" I said, ignoring the idea of not having my Father around anymore. Before I could stop it, a few tears started rolling down my face and I argued, "You just don't care as much as I do! Nobody does... I just wish someone cared as much as I do."

CHAPTER SEVEN
THE DATE
STANTON HIGH SCHOOL PARKING LOT
WEDNESDAY, MAY 23RD
5 PM

I wasn't sure what came over me in Chief Ramzorin's office, but now I was done with crying.

Unfortunately, to the fullest extent, Donovan was my ride back to my car at the high school. On a better note, he didn't know that I cried in Chief Ramzorin's office, so he couldn't make fun of me, for now.

Instead, we drove along the Stanton Stretch back to the high school in a golden silence. I never looked over at Donovan, but finally being in the passenger seat instead of being the driver, I was able to look out and watch everything around us. That's when I noticed Mrs. Traven's bakery was closing down, and I started up a conversation to show I didn't hate him. Also, he sounded like he was on my side when I first proposed the idea, and I needed as much help as I could get.

"Huh, Mrs. Traven's bakery is closing," I mentioned.

Donovan looked over quickly as he approached the stop light in the middle of Stanton Stretch so he could turn left into the school zone.

"Oh, that's sad. I remember going there when I was your age," Donovan commented.

"You did?" I asked. "How long have you lived out here?"

"You really want to know?"

"Well, I think we got off on the wrong foot, so yeah, let's start relating and bonding, shall we?" I mocked.

Donovan sneered back at me and said, "Yeah, I have lived here a while. My parents hated me and wanted me to move out right when I was eighteen, so I picked a place and they showered me with money, only in the hopes that they'd never have to see me again. I was eighteen years old and I paid for my house in cash. The realtor was baffled and wondered how that could ever be possible. I wasn't as personal with the realtor as I'm being with you though, so she never heard the real story."

"Why did your parents hate you?"

"Because I wasn't the gifted son they had hoped for, I guess? I wanted to do something with my life that they didn't want me to do. They wanted a son who'd be a doctor or in some kind of orchestra, but let's face it; I sucked at the game Operation and I sucked at blowing into an instrument, so they gave up and just gave me hell until the day I turned eighteen, and I was out, with a bunch of their money. They just wanted me to go away."

"That's pretty messed up," I said, not ever knowing much about Donovan's past. "I'm sorry."

"Don't mention it, Jack. I guess being a cop just wasn't Ivy League enough for my parents."

"And then, with Billy's parents..."

"Yeah," Donovan started. "See, my parents were on the richer side of the family while the other brothers and sisters of my Father were on a more middle-class side, which included Billy and his parents. Finally, I was able to come to one of their little reunions that I never got to go to when I was younger, about five... or has it been six... years ago, I saw Billy's parents trying to score money for crack from everyone else. If I would've been in jurisdiction, I would've cuffed both of them and sent them away in a heartbeat, but instead, I saw the hurt look in Billy's eyes and I decided I had to take him in, and later I reported his parents to the authorities in their city."

I remembered Billy moving to Stanton at the beginning of sixth grade. No one remembered him from elementary school, so a lot of questions were brought upon him, which made him get upset pretty easily. He didn't like being taken away from his parents until he got older and realized what was best for him.

I still felt bad for Billy, just like he felt bad for me when everything happened with my dad in ninth grade. We were there for each other both times, and that's why we connected. I wondered now why we weren't so close anymore. That's just high school, I guess.

"So, his parents are locked up now?" I asked.

"Yeah, good riddance," Donovan replied.

"I was really good friends with Billy up until about tenth grade. I'm not sure what happened, but we just kinda drifted away."

"You guys should hang out sometime before graduation. He always talks about how you are and stuff," Donovan mentioned.

"He does?" I asked. "I mean, he talked to me briefly yesterday, asking how I was, but I didn't really think much of it."

"Yeah, he misses you, Jack. A lot of people seem to like you, but I haven't found out why," Donovan said with a smile going across his face.

"Screw you," I replied after laughing softly.

We were now close to the high school parking lot and Donovan replied, "Hey, I'm on duty, you can't talk to me like that."

We both laughed, letting our petty differences from before subside and letting the things we had in common come to the table.

Donovan was pretty cool I guess. He made his way on his own. Well, maybe not entirely on his own, but his parents paid for him to leave. I'm not sure how I would feel if that happened to me... hate-filled or full of freedom?

But right when we pulled into the parking lot, Donovan stopped the car and said, "I'll let you walk to your car so you can get some exercise."

"I don't know if I need exercise as much as a cop who probably drinks coffee with doughnut bits floating around in it," I answered as I opened the door.

"Really didn't see that one coming, Jack," Donovan argued playfully, but then, as I stepped out, he added, "Jack, hold on a second. I just wanted to say I'm sorry for being an angry cuss back at the station, it's just... I really have a passion for detective work, and when you come in saying that I didn't do my job, it pisses me off a little bit, naturally. But if you do find anything on a possible killer for Sam, not saying you should pursue it, but if you continue to, since I know teens rebel, then you should share it with me or the Chief, okay?"

"Okay," I said, happy at the fact that someone new and more powerful was now on my side. But with the final joke, I ended, "If I find something, you can be my backup."

Leaving Donovan in the police cruiser laughing, I walked out of the car and closed the door the best I could without slamming it. As soon as it closed, he sped off and left me alone in the almost completely empty parking lot.

Only a few cars remained, but the majority of them were close together in the middle of the parking lot. It was probably a group of friends who had an after-school club.

Mine was towards the front by the sidewalk, and I saw a familiar vehicle sitting beside mine.

Alyssa's.

Was she waiting for me this whole time?

Only one way to find out.

I started walking up to our cars and I had an eerie feeling about how empty the parking lot was. But, it reminded me of when I just had my permit and my mom helped me learn to drive and park in the school parking lot. That's what most kids did, and it worked.

As I stepped up next to the trunk of my car, I slowed down to see if Alyssa was in her car. She was, with the windows just barely cracked and her eyes closed. I remembered her telling me when we first started dating that if she had the chance to take a nap, she took it. One day, she followed me around with my Mom at a furniture store so we could buy a new couch in my living room and she took a chance by taking a nap on one of the sofas. And no, this wasn't just some two-second nap, she literally stayed on the one couch we already looked at and fell asleep.

When I pulled her off, she seemed mad that I disturbed her slumber, but I didn't care. We got a bunch of funny looks from the staff the rest of the time we were there.

"Alyssa?" I said, trying to get her attention.

She moved around a little in her seat, but she wasn't awake yet, so I tried again. This time, just a little louder.

"Alyssa!"

She jumped, hit her knees on the steering wheel, and tried raising the roof with her dainty arms. Gasping for air, she looked over at me and said, "Jack! There you are."

She started to open her door and I stepped over to the backseat doors to let her step out. God, why did she look so great all the time?

"Yeah, sorry for waking you up," I said as she started to face me.

"The dream was kinda boring anyway, one I've had before," she answered. "So, what happened at the police station?"

"Well, I got my ass chewed, to say the least. I'm supposed to stop looking for a killer."

"Supposed to?" Alyssa asked. "So, you're saying you're not?"

"No, why would I stop looking? I haven't even looked at all of the possible ideas."

"Jack," she started.

"Are you telling me to give up?"

"No, just, do you have something else?"

"Not yet…"

"Then just slow down a little bit, that's all I'm asking," Alyssa said.

"Okay…" I replied reluctantly. "But, why did you wait here for me?"

"I said I would, didn't I?"

"Well, yeah, I'm not saying you're not a person of your word, I just don't see why you couldn't just text me or call me or something."

"Because I wanted to be formal with you," Alyssa answered in a sweet tone.

"That's nice of you."

"I thought so too. So, how about you and me go out to Victor's Diner for dinner?"

She was very forward and more confident than ever about the idea.

"Dinner… tonight?" I asked to clarify.

"Yeah, just you and me, and dinner. So, how about it?"

"I'd have to ask my Mom I guess…"

"Okay, well tell me when she says yes and then I'll be picking you up at seven."

"You're picking me up?"

"Yeah, I invited you."

"I know, but…"

"Look, Jack, this is a treat for you since you're going through a rough time. Just accept it."

"I'm not arguing about it," I explained. "You just… surprised me, that's all."

"I like surprising people. Makes me feel like I have the upper hand or something," Alyssa said back with a wink that I didn't know if it was innocent or not. "I'll see you then."

She got back in her car and started it before I could even step out of the way. Once I headed over to the driver's side, she pulled away and waved as she drove off.

So, I had a date, with my ex-girlfriend. What could go wrong?

*****

When I texted my Mom to ask if I could go, she texted back, "A million times, yes!"

So many people kept egging me on to go for her again and make amends and blah, blah, blah. They all acted like our relationship was some broken love story that could be fixed so easily. But hey, maybe they were right.

We ended on an argument that I don't even remember now, that brought out the worst of both of us and broke us up when we were at our weakest. (No, I'm not trying to be the dramatic teenager, although if I was being one, you wouldn't still be reading this).

Anyway, ever since then people complained to me and asked "What went wrong" and "Who broke up with who", even though I knew they didn't really care and they just liked the Dirty Laundry. Don Henley knew what that was all about.

Sadly, it was a song that Alyssa had shown me. Dammit... I guess she really impacted me in one year a little more than most people did in my entire lifetime.

So, I started trying to smell better and tidying up my image by wearing a sleek black polo and some darker jeans that I had paid a little more for than my other jeans. I thought of it as a date, and I didn't want to ask Alyssa how she was dressing when I texted her back that I could go, so I dressed up a little bit just in case.

Alyssa texted back, "Okay, I'll be there at seven."

I hoped by "there" she meant my house, otherwise, I was going to get stood up just as fast as I was set down.

All I could think about while getting ready was the night after the bowling alley and a few of our other memories, and I started feeling sad, or maybe it was just reminiscent. I don't know... I hoped tonight would go well... but not too well.

Just as I sprayed on a little bit of cologne, my doorbell rang for the first time in ages and I went downstairs to open it, wondering why my mom wasn't home yet. But maybe it was better that way.

When I opened the door, I saw Alyssa standing by the threshold and she looked so great... as usual. She wore a loose black blouse and tight jeans that distracted me, along with high top boots. Some would've thought it was an odd combination on someone else, but it worked perfectly for Alyssa. Now I understood why Nick was always so fixated on her.

"Hi, Jack," she said, trying to lure me into her booby trap... literally.

But I tried to play it cool like before and I replied, "Hey, Alyssa, are we all ready to go?"

"Ready if you are," she replied.

"Yup, so let's go."

We started walking to her car and she made her way over to the driver's seat. She had pulled up next to the curb, which seemed to be her favorite spot, and just as she unlocked the doors, she warned, "Watch your step."

I knew she was referring to the night of the bowling alley where we first met.

"Ha-ha," I said.

We piled into her car and she started it while flicking the front lights on, which wasn't really needed that badly, but it was a good precaution. Now that it was almost summer the sun stayed out longer, but because of the engulfing forest, we were always kind of left in the dark.

Alyssa pulled away from the curb safely and made a U-turn to head out to the Stanton Stretch. On the way there, she kept talking to me.

"What have you been up to?" she asked.

"Anticipating the end of high school I guess," I answered, "you?"

"Same, and looking forward to college."

"Oh yeah? Where are you going to college at?"

"I got offered two half scholarships, but both are out of state."

"Half scholarships?"

"Yeah, where they only pay tuition and maybe a few books."

"That sucks," I commented.

"It's better than nothing. My grandparents were thrilled when they got the letters in the mail."

"I bet so."

"Any college for you, Jack?"

"I don't know… I was going to go with Sam to wherever he went to, but…"

Alyssa scowled at the situation and how everything was, and she tried to make me feel better with some consolation.

"Jack, I'm really sorry about all of that."

"No, I'm sorry for bringing it up. You probably already hear a lot about it from Emily."

"She does talk about it a lot, but she also says that she knew they wouldn't last."

"Wait, what?" I asked, and I knew if I had been driving and Alyssa said that, I would've slammed on the brakes.

But Alyssa just nodded sadly and continued, "She said Sam wasn't really being himself as much in the last few days before... Yeah... And now she feels bad for even thinking it would end."

"How was Sam not being himself?"

"She just said he was down about things... Now she feels responsible for his suicide, which is why she broke down when you thought it might've been murder."

"Oh," I said, and I thought about Sam and Emily breaking up. Honestly, I couldn't see it. They were so happy together, and now, I thought maybe that's why Sam would've killed himself because he knew they were going to break up. Or... Alyssa did say that Sam was sad before he even committed suicide, so maybe he knew what was coming for him...

Without saying another word to one another, we made it to Victor's Diner on the north edge of town and we walked in after finding a pretty close parking spot. When we stepped in, it almost seemed like nobody else was there, but the waiter explained they weren't very busy on Wednesday nights. So, I guess Alyssa and I just looked like a bunch of hungry Atheists, which didn't even really bother me that much.

Once we were seated at a table just across from a few booths that were occupied by some burly looking men who were watching a football game, the waiter handed us our menus and walked off, leaving Alyssa and me alone again.

She was afraid to talk again, I knew she was. I was speechless for the most part, but not in a good way. Otherwise, I would've said something.

"Did you decide what you want?" the waiter asked before even bringing us our drinks. I guess we really didn't look that talkative so he just wanted to hurry us out.

But, Alyssa said, "You just handed us the menus about two minutes ago."

"Oh, I'm sorry guys, I'm just not used to this lag," the waiter explained. "I'll be back with your drinks soon."

The waiter walked off and Alyssa shook her head in an irritated way.

"I've had this waiter before. He's a real hoot."

"I can tell," I said, knowing that even though it was Taco Night, I would play it safe by ordering a burger.

"Jack, if you don't mind, I'd rather you don't talk to Emily about the whole, 'they might've broken up before the suicide' thing."

"Yeah, don't worry; I'm not one to blab."

"I know you're not, but just to be safe, I thought I'd ask."

"I understand."

Alyssa shuffled around in her seat, knowing what she wanted. Her menu was down on the table, but I only had mine up so I didn't seem weird staring at her. But since she was staring at me, I put my menu down and stared right back.

"Any more leads?" Alyssa asked.

"No. But we have a few more members to our little group," I informed.

Just as Alyssa started to ask deeper into that, the waiter came back with our drinks and asked what we'd like to have to eat. I ordered a mushroom and Swiss burger while Alyssa ordered the blackened chicken salad with their signature ranch. The waiter took the menus away and got out of the way.

"Like who?" Alyssa asked.

I took a drink from my Coke and replied, "Harold Vero, Mark Collins, and Nick Wallace."

"Why them?"

"Harold kept asking about what happened with Emily, and you know how Mark and Nick always tag along with him, so of course they were interested."

"What did they say?"

"They suggested that maybe it was jealousy. Gregory Allen wanted to be the quarterback this year but Sam got it instead."

"That's true, but as much as I hate Gregory Allen, I don't think he'd do that," Alyssa contrasted.

"Yeah, I didn't really think so either. Gregory's more of an all talk kinda guy."

"And Ben told me about how you thought it might've been Jessica Pivlett, which actually didn't seem so irrational, except that she lives in Maine now."

"Yeah, that was another idea that went down the drain."

"And it definitely wasn't the parents…?"

"No, there's no way the Millers did it. They're just too great of parents, and they have an alibi."

"Damn," Alyssa cursed.

"I know, but I'm actually glad it's none of those people," I answered.

"Yeah," Alyssa agreed.

We both drank down the rest of our drinks and then the waiter came by at the ready with the refills. Once we started to drink those in silence, Alyssa gave me a look and I asked, "What?"

She stopped drinking her water and she asked, "Well, what if I don't know who did it, but I have an idea of what happened that night?"

"By all means, share," I requested, pushing my drink aside.

"Bear with me," she started, and I could tell she was nervous to share her idea. "Have you ever heard of partner suicide?"

"No, I haven't," I answered honestly in confusion. "What is it?"

"I thought of it the other day when I found out you were looking for a killer... basically, it's when two people convince each other to kill themselves together so they don't feel so alone. I saw a story on it a few years ago on TV and I shuddered. Some guy was finding lonely women in chat rooms online and then convincing them to kill themselves in front of a camera while he watched. A few of them, he tricked into thinking that he was going to too, but he was sentenced to ninety years in prison on four counts of murder."

"So you're saying," I started, with a sick feeling coming over me again.

"Sam did commit suicide, but with someone else."

"And that 'someone else' didn't pull the trigger," I finished.

"Exactly," Alyssa said. "Otherwise, why would've Sam done it? Maybe it was Sam's final act of, being the nice guy?"

"But the other person just set him up to where Sam was the only one to kill himself," I said, angry at the thought of it.

Alyssa nodded.

Now we had how it was pulled off, just not a person or a reason why. That was enough for me to still be confident in finding the killer.

But soon after finishing the conversation, the waiter brought out our food and we started eating to try and not think about Sam and murder too much. At first, I just nibbled on the fries, a little sickened from what we had talked about, but eventually, I devoured the burger and fries and Alyssa took out a chunk of her salad to where there wasn't enough to take home in a to-go box.

Finally, the waiter brought the check and business started to get a little busier just before we were about to leave.

Pulling out my wallet, I started sifting through the bills and I noticed I had a lot more money than I remembered. I had about one hundred fifty-three dollars in twenties and ones.

But, Alyssa glared at me and said, "Why do you have your wallet out? I'm paying."

She pulled out a handbag that I didn't even notice before. I guess I was too busy looking at... other things.

Anyway, the argument that I could see from a mile away started.

"No, no, no, I ordered a drink and a pretty expensive burger, I'd feel bad," I urged.

"Well I invited you and I am trying to treat you so stop it and let me pay."

She gave me a look that I hadn't seen in a while and that meant I needed to stop and count my losses.

"Okay, you can pay while I run to the bathroom, that way it seems as though you beat me to it," I said as I started standing up.

"Deal," she replied, and I walked off.

On the way to the bathroom, I saw one of the burly men watching the game stand up as well needing to pee, which didn't surprise me, seeing that all of the men at the booth had about two large mugs of beer each in the time Alyssa and I had eaten.

When I walked into the bathroom, I saw no one else was in there and I headed for the stall to ease my unreasonable fear of public bathrooms. I don't really know when it started, I just never liked them, and I liked a box around me.

The man had walked in too, but I figured he'd just use a urinal.

I did my business, thinking about how surprisingly well this night was going. Alyssa wasn't mad at me, we were on talking terms, and she paid for my meal. I'd say that it's a home run.

But when I stepped out of the stall and the automatic toilet flushed behind me, I saw the big man standing right by the door and he was kind of in my way. His beard ran down farther than any drool that has ever left my mouth and he didn't seem too happy. I guess he needed to do number two.

"Hey, sorry, I didn't know you needed this one—"

Before I could even finish what I was saying or process what was happening, the man lunged at me and sent me into the wall. Back in the stall, I hit my back against the handlebar of the stall and looked back up to see him coming for me again. Right as he was about to hit me, I tried striking him with my shoulder and the side of my head to his torso but he only barely backed up. A few jabs came into my side and I struggled to keep myself up, so I hit back a few times as hard as I could. This guy wasn't budging though, and he kept punching me.

Finally, I decided to break away, but now the guy wouldn't let me go, and instead, he put me in a chokehold with my head dug into his stomach. I gasped for air, scared of what would happen next. It got so bad that I couldn't breathe at all, so I took a desperate measure and pulled out my knife with my right hand and flicked it open. As soon as it flipped open, I struck the blade against his arm and he cried out in pain and let me go.

I fell back against the wall for the last time and the man looked up at me, holding his arm to try and stop the bleeding. My heart pounded harder than ever against my chest and I watched his blood drip off my knife.

The man grunted as he stood over the toilet, and before he could lunge one more time, I attempted a half-assed karate kick into his throat. The move made the man crumple to the ground and gasp for air.

"Freeze!" Donovan yelled at us as he barged into the bathroom, pistol drawn.

I looked at Donovan and he fast-walked over with his gun pointed down.

As soon as he saw the assailant, Donovan lifted the pistol once more and the man put his hands up and against the wall. Then, Donovan glanced at me.

"You okay, Jack?"

As I wiped a little blood from my lip with my left hand, I replied, "Never been better."

CHAPTER EIGHT
THE LAST PIECE
VICTOR'S DINER
WEDNESDAY, MAY 23RD
8:25 PM

Every cop in the town decided to check-in and see what happened at the usually friendly diner.

The parade of red and blue lights flashing in the parking lot would've given even a person with no medical history of seizures their first one. An ambulance helped look me over while another one on the other side of the parking lot bandaged the man who tried to... well, I really had no idea what he was trying to do.

Donovan and Alyssa stood by me at the ambulance while I got my quick fix. Alyssa was worried sick about me, even though I was sitting right in front of her.

Then, I asked the question that ran through my mind right when Donovan busted through the bathroom door.

"How did you know what was happening?" I asked Donovan.

"Chief Ramzorin ordered for me to tail you for the night; he said he had a bad feeling," Donovan explained calmly.

"Well he was right," I answered.

Right when the man who attacked me started to be escorted by another police officer to the backseat of a police cruiser, I asked, "What was he even trying to do?"

"He admitted that he mugged you, or at least, tried," Donovan said. "You put up a helluva fight, Jack. I heard you guys tussling from out in the bar."

"I'm glad you heard what was happening," I said.

"I don't think it would've really mattered if I wasn't here. You knifed him pretty badly and gave him a good kick. Where'd you learn to defend yourself like that?"

Donovan and Alyssa both waited for my answer, but I knew they weren't too thrilled about it once I said it.

"My Dad taught me how to fight when I was younger, and Sam taught me some stuff too."

To try and make light of the situation, Donovan said, "They'd be proud of you from how you handled yourself."

"I guess so," I replied.

Before I found out the man was just trying to mug me, I thought maybe he was Sam's killer, who was now coming for me. But that'd just be weird if he ended up being the one.

I now remembered trying to pay for the meal, and I did kind of flash my money around to where everyone could see it, so I guess he wanted to take advantage of the situation. He could afford a beer or two, but nothing else, so he had to steal it from a kid.

Actually, I wasn't really a kid anymore, according to the law.

"So, you're okay?" Chief Ramzorin asked as he appeared from the night.

"Why're you out here?" I asked.

"Same reason everyone else is. We don't see much action around here, do we, Donovan?" Chief Ramzorin explained, looking at Donovan.

"No, but you were also worried about Jack, weren't you?" Donovan asked.

"Yes, you got me. Right when I heard about it, I called all units to the diner. That part was my mistake I guess."

"Well, thanks for watching out for me, but I don't really like being followed," I said.

"I guess we don't need to anymore, now that my bad feeling has gone away," Chief Ramzorin commented.

Then, to make the date even worse, my Mom came running through the hordes of people to come see her little baby, which, by the way, that's me.

"Oh my God, Jack!" she started, racing over to hug me. But before she did, she froze and went, "Wait, I can hug you, right? You don't have any broken ribs...?"

"No, Mom, I'm fine," I replied.

As soon as I told her that, she jumped in and gave me a warm hug. I hugged back but watched Alyssa smile in the background while the hug continued.

"Your son put up a good fight," Donovan said.

My Mom let go of me and looked at Donovan with a surprised look.

"Really? Sounds like my son. I think we've had enough excitement for one night. Let's go home, Jack."

My Mom started to walk away and I looked at Alyssa with a sorry face, but she said "No" softly and my Mom noticed Alyssa.

"Oh, yeah, sorry Jack, I forgot you were on a date!" my Mom announced. "Well, just meet me back at the house then, okay?"

"Okay Mom, love you," I said, smiling at Alyssa as my Mom walked off to her car.

"Love you too."

When my Mom was gone, I stepped out the back of the ambulance and started toward Alyssa, but Chief Ramzorin intervened and said, "So, you sure you're all right, Jack?"

"Yes, I'm good," I said, a little annoyed from the whole ordeal. I really just wanted to go home, but only after I talked to Alyssa some more.

"Okay, well you kids drive safe and Jack, don't brag too much about this at school," Chief Ramzorin warned me.

"Don't worry; I doubt anyone will even really mention it."

Alyssa and I walked back to her car and we were off pretty soon after that, but it did take a while to navigate through the other police cars. Soon enough, we were cruising down the Stanton Stretch back to my house so we could part ways, but she wasn't letting me go that easily.

"Jack?"

"Yes?" I replied as I looked out at the small shops I had grown up with all my life.

"What happened at the restaurant... it really scared me."

"Alyssa—"

"No Jack, I'm serious. I can't believe that man was going to mug you after choking you to death."

"He just put me in a headlock for just a few seconds," I argued.

"Just? You're acting like this happens to you all the time!"

"Calm down, Alyssa. You're speeding."

She looked over at the speedometer and realized I was right, so she slowed down and took a deep breath. I did too.

"I care about you, Jack, a lot more than you think."

"I'm pretty sure I know how much you care about me," I replied. "I heard about Shakey's."

"What about it?"

"Oh don't even try to play it off. Everyone kept harassing me on

Monday about how you droned on and on about me and that you were worried about me."

"Okay, maybe I talked about you a little more than I should've," Alyssa admitted, "but I wasn't the only one, okay?"

"Yeah, but you talked the most about me."

Wiping away a tear that I didn't see coming, she argued, "Well maybe I just missed you, that's all."

I felt bad for making her cry, which would make three women in one week. God, I prayed there wouldn't be a fourth.

"Alyssa... C'mon, don't be like that. You think I didn't miss you?"

"Seems like you don't," she replied. "We haven't talked in a long time until this all happened."

"It's been a year," I corrected.

"That's a long time for me. We used to talk every day and then... Boom! No more texts or calls or funny pictures throughout the day, it was such a random shift."

"I... didn't think we should keep talking. It just made me think things would be harder. You were my first serious girlfriend; I didn't know what to do!"

"What?" she asked, seeming surprised. "I thought... you never told me that."

"Well it's true, okay? I'm the loser who lost my Dad and never had a real girlfriend because most people thought I was a freak, and then Sam set you up to be my first serious girlfriend, which then I lose over a stupid argument that I bet neither of us can remember, and then I lose my best friend."

"I remember what it was about..."

I turned to Alyssa as she wiped away the tears from her face. Now, I didn't feel so bad. It almost seemed like Alyssa's tears were saved from what had happened, and not what was happening now.

"We compared our relationship to Sam and Emily's, and then we asked which one was better. You said ours was, but I expected that... so I tried to argue for Sam and Emily's side, by pointing out small things that went wrong in our relationship, but you took it too personally. So you asked what else you had done wrong, and I said there was nothing, but you kept thinking there was something else... I never said what it was though, and so you started telling me things that I did wrong and it really hurt me, so we argued for another hour until finally, you suggested breaking up and we did."

The story came flying back into my memory and my face felt hot. My eyes started watering and I felt like I bit into a jalapeño right off the vine. It hurt to remember how childish I was about the argument, but I guess that was true for both of us. We argued about something that didn't need to be argued. If it wasn't for that, we would still be together...

With her brakes squeaking, I noticed we were back at my house by the curb and it was my time to leave. I looked at Alyssa but she stared down and continued to rub her eyes clear.

"I'm sorry, I didn't mean to make you cry. I'll leave you alone now. Thanks for dinner."

I was trying to make a quick getaway not because she was crying, but because I felt like I wasn't needed anymore. Not by her, or really anyone else. So, I decided to step out and walk back into my house and go to bed early.

But then, something else happened.

"Jack..."

And right when I turned around, she was there, kissing me with my door open and the night breeze whisking its way into the car, but we didn't even really feel it. The kiss provided a warmth that nothing else could've.

Once we separated and I looked at her with the dumbest look I could've, she said, *"We can work it out."*

Again, someone in my life had quoted a song to explain how everything in life was going to go. Sam was right when he quoted The White Stripes, and now Alyssa was right when she quoted The Beatles. We could work it out, but not tonight.

I smiled, and with that, she let me leave her car and walk into my house to end our evening together, which was an evening that was postponed for too long.

"So, how'd it go besides the mugger?"

My Mom walked up to me from upstairs and I answered, "It was... good."

"Just good?" my mom asked.

"Yeah, just, good," I said, and I started to walk up the stairs to my room with a blushing face.

"We'll talk about it later, right?" my Mom asked eagerly.

But I crushed her dreams by answering, "Goodnight, Mom."

*****

The next morning on Thursday, May 24th, I went to school for what I thought would be a short day but turned out to be a lot longer than I wanted it to be.

In third hour, Sociology, Gregory Allen decided to give me kudos for what happened at Victor's Diner.

"Hey, watch out guys, I hear Jack can really take care of himself," Gregory warned everyone.

"Why, what happened?" Kelsey Stokes asked, a girl who was very sweet and smart, but said the dumbest things.

"Jack was about to get mugged, but he doesn't take shit from no one," Gregory said, and I felt my face get red.

Mr. Tinley perked up and scolded, "Hey, watch your language. You all might be seniors, but I can still write discipline referrals."

"Well I'm serious Mr. Tinley; Jack used a knife on this guy who wouldn't stop trying to knock him out in a headlock."

Mr. Tinley looked at me and asked, "No shit? Seriously?"

Everyone laughed and I even joined in. Afterward, I had to explain the story to everyone and I got a few girls to start looking at me in a "more-than-a-friend" way, but it was too late. Another girl had my heart, or is that too corny?

But by the end of the hour, I didn't think that Gregory would've killed Sam. Gregory was a jerk, but he wouldn't go that far with something. Now, he was checked off of the list of possibilities and I was back at having zero.

*****

I don't want to mention what happened in every hour because nothing really important happened. But if you're still interested, here's a mini explanation: In fourth hour, Government, Emily and I worked together again but this time she didn't hold my hand. Instead, she kept talking about a senior trip she was wanting to take with Alyssa and maybe a few other girls. It sounded fun, but I knew she didn't want me to come along. I never even thought about taking a senior trip. If I did take one, I would've wanted to go with Sam somewhere. He always talked about seeing the Rock and Roll Hall of Fame in Cleveland, Ohio. Maybe I'd just go there in his memory.

*****

Fifth hour, Humanities, we didn't watch a video or do a pointless worksheet, but instead, we sat around all hour and just talked about stuff. A few people walked up to me and asked what happened last night. Alyssa told the story to a few people in a very majestic way and then she winked at me when they walked away. I smiled back.

*****

At lunch, I sat by the "Nerd Herd" and we talked about, well, video games. Eventually, I told Nick how I scored with Alyssa last night and he almost had a heart attack.

"Are you serious!?" Nick practically shouted.

We got a few weird looks from some other people and I had to calm him down.

"Yes, but don't go telling a bunch of people," I ordered.

"Aw, c'mon Jack. You can't tell me something that great and then tell me not to tell anyone," Nick complained.

"I'm serious. If anyone finds out, I'm coming for you."

"He's serious too," Harold kidded. "He'll cut you up, Nick."

"Oh yeah, I heard about that," Mark said. "What happened?"

"Well… I tried to be gentlemanly and pay for the meal, but I ended up tipping off some guy that I had a bunch of money so he jumped me in the bathroom."

"Wait, so you really cut the guy?" Nick asked, a little scared from Harold's threat earlier.

"Yeah, I did. He wouldn't let go."

"It was life or death," Harold said, "and Jack happily chose life, and now he's here to share the tale."

"I'm trying to decide which one is more exciting… knifing some guy who tried to mug you, or…"

Nick stopped to stand up and I couldn't believe what he was about to do. He stood up on his chair and yelled, "Or when Jack Sampson kissed Alyssa Jackson last night after their date!"

I stared at Nick, dumbfounded. Someone on the far end of the commons started clapping and a few others joined in until the whole cafeteria was filled with claps and cheers for my "win".

I shook my head and lowered it in embarrassment but Harold patted my back and said it was okay. I looked up at Nick and he had a big smile on his face.

"I am going to kill you," I said through the awkward laughing.

"Well wait until after school, I still have a few more people to tell," Nick said boldly.

I didn't really hate Nick for shouting that, but I guess I just didn't really care anymore. I wasn't ashamed of kissing Alyssa; I just didn't know what she thought about the whole thing. Honestly, she probably felt the same as me, which made me happy.

What was once a moment I didn't think way too much of, I now thought that maybe Alyssa kissing me was some defining moment of... something. The end to senior year, sort of an ultimate ending?

But we still had a few more days to go. I was just being too hopeful about everything.

*****

Seventh hour, Journalism, for once, we had a different assignment.

"Now I know I've made this really easy for you guys this year," Mrs. Waverly admitted, "but now I've got a fun one for you guys."

A few kids groaned, not really crazy about the idea of doing something else from the usual read a story and then interpret the goods and bads.

"Well, you've been reading over a bunch of articles this semester so now you should know how to write one. I want you guys to write a story, only two people in a group together, and I don't care if it's a true story or you make something up, but it must be school appropriate."

"School appropriate" was a joke. If the teachers actually heard what most of the students talked about, "School appropriate" would never be used as a standard for an assignment.

I was always that kid who just remained seated when everyone else got up to find a partner. Usually, I was eventually approached by someone who just wanted to use me for my smarts, but this time was different. Everyone else in the room found a partner except for me and...

Billy Young.

We made eye contact only for a second, realizing we were the only two losers with no partner. So, he motioned me over to him in a nice way and I accepted the offer.

Pulling up a desk to him, he turned to face me with a piece of paper and a pencil.

"I'll write if you tell the story," Billy offered.

"Okay... What story do I tell?"

"I would say the one from last night, but you're probably tired of that."

"Did Donovan tell you about it?"

Billy nodded.

"He was surprised you put up such a fight, but then I mentioned the movie theater story with you and Sam…"

He stopped and looked at me.

"I'm… sorry."

"About what?" I asked.

"Mentioning Sam."

"Oh, it's no big deal. It's a happy memory," I replied.

Billy barely smiled, happy that I wasn't upset from what he said. Why would I be? Sam was my best friend, and everyone knew the story. Except for Donovan, I guess.

"What did Donovan say?" I asked.

"About the movie theater story? Oh, nothing really. Just that it made sense once he saw you break free from that guy at the diner."

"Oh, okay," I answered.

We went quiet for a second, until Billy said, "Hey, you know what; I don't think I ever apologized for not going to the movie with you."

"You didn't?"

"No… Actually, I don't even think I told you why I couldn't go," Billy added. "Gary's car actually broke down when he was trying to start it at his house, and his parents weren't home, so we just stayed there."

"Why didn't you call me or Sam?" I asked.

"Gary suggested that, but I hate to bum rides off of people. But I wish I could've gone. I heard those kids from Warren really had it coming for them."

"Yeah, they kept making fun of my haircut, which is why I thought you didn't go," I told him.

"Oh, no man, I'm not that shallow. Or was I?"

"Maybe a little bit," I said honestly.

"Oh, well sorry about that."

"It's okay."

We sat in silence for another minute or two until I saw the time was really going by faster than I thought. All the other kids were talking and discussing stories. I heard one kid talking about aliens taking over our small town just for the hell of it.

"So, do you want to do that?" Billy asked.

"Do what?" I replied.

"Y'know, a story about your little squabble last night."

111

"Oh, I guess so, if that doesn't seem too conceited."

Billy smiled at an idea.

"Well hey; maybe we could make it funnier by making it conceited. We'll exaggerate the story like crazy and make you seem ten feet tall."

"Ha-ha, yeah, okay!" I said.

So, I told Billy the story and he exaggerated it as he wrote it down. It reminded me of back when we were best friends, and how we were always laughing around each other. I think Mrs. Waverly looked over at us a few times, surprised to see that I was laughing and enjoying life again.

I still missed Sam, and I still intended to catch the killer, but for now, I just let the good times roll.

Toward the end of the hour, Mrs. Waverly decided to surprise us by saying that we had to read our stories aloud to the other classmates. Billy and I looked at each other and started laughing and pointing fingers. I definitely didn't want to read it because of how crazy Billy had made the story. And luckily, the whole class kept arguing until the bell rang and everyone was released. Billy and I headed toward the parking lot of the high school, talking about random things.

"Oh, but I talked to Donovan and got to know him a little more than I used to," I said.

"Do you regret it now?" Billy asked, pulling a smirk out.

"Not really, he had some interesting things to say, especially how his parents paid him to move out."

"Yeah, that was pretty crazy to me too," Billy agreed. "Did he say anything about me?"

"No… Well, he said you missed me."

"I hope he clarified I meant only like a friend," Billy said. "I know I haven't had a girlfriend in a while, but I'm not, you know."

"Yeah, I know you're not, but at one point I really got my hopes up," I said, sticking my tongue out and laughing.

He joined in with me, and then the laughter subsided and Billy asked, "Hey, we should hang out before senior year is over and everyone flies off into their happily ever afters."

"That sounds pretty fun," I said. "How about a movie?"

We both laughed at that, and then he started walking away from me without even noticing it, but when he did he asked, "Oh, I'm parked over there. Talk to you tomorrow?"

"Yeah, maybe we can BS some other story," I said hopefully.

"Sounds good. See ya, Jack."

Billy headed over to his Ford F-150 extended cab and started it up. I walked over to my car and saw Ben standing by it. He looked a little hurt that I didn't find him and walk with him, but hey, one broken friendship at a time.

"Jack, I was looking for you earlier since we weren't able to talk in first hour," Ben said.

"Well I'm sorry, we can talk now. Is it about Gregory?"

"Yes, it is. But it's not good news."

"Maybe you should define good news first," I said.

Ben hesitated, and then realized I was joking. Then he said, "I don't think it's him."

"Why not?"

"He's just, not that kind of jerk, you know? He's probably still bitter about it, but he did go to Shakey's and say some good things about Sam after putting his usual attitude to the side."

"Yeah, Alyssa didn't think it was him either," I replied. "And today, he was bragging about how I fended off that attacker at the diner, and he was complimenting me."

"Just because he might've hated Sam doesn't mean he hates you," Ben explained, but then asked, "What happened there, by the way?"

"I just attracted the wrong person," I said simply.

"How?"

"Well, Alyssa took me on a little date last night and I offered to pay at the end of it, and I forgot how much money was in my wallet so I ended up flashing around a bunch of twenties and he must've seen it."

"Oh," Ben said. "But, you're okay?"

"Yes, I'm okay. He ended up getting hurt, not me."

"I know but, you've had a lot happen to you in the past few days, so I wanted to make sure."

"Yeah, Ben, I'm good," I said, and then I glanced at my watch. "Hey, you should probably get going, or else you'll have to bribe your sister again."

"Oh! Thanks, Jack, see you later!" Ben thanked as he headed for his car.

I shook my head, wanting to laugh at how tightly Ben was wound around his dad's finger, but I guess it'd end up making Ben a better person in the end.

What kind of person was I going to end up as after high school? Some washed up, depressed loser who couldn't forget about what happened with his best friend? Maybe. Or, I should just stop thinking about stuff so much and just let life happen the way it was meant to. I believed in fate, for the most part. The only part I didn't believe about fate was that Sam had to die. Not as young as he did, at least.

*****

I got home earlier than usual at about three fifteen and I had nothing to do. So, I tried entertaining myself with my computer and texting a few people, but nothing seemed to really be happening, so I'll save you the boring details.

Eventually, I wondered when my mom was going to be home. It turned seven thirty and I checked my phone to see if I missed any texts from her. After waiting for a little bit, I got a call from her and I answered.

"Hello?" I said.

"Jack, honey, I'm really sorry, something came up at work and I'm having to stay overtime. Looks like everyone else decided to take a four day weekend except for me, so I can't be home to make dinner," my Mom said, out of breath.

"Oh, that's okay Mom, I'll just go get something to eat," I replied.

"Well, I hate to ask you to do things, but would you mind going to the store for me? There's a list on the fridge and I marked where everything should be. If you could?"

"Yeah, sure Mom, don't worry about it."

"Oh, thanks, sweetie. I'll try to be home as soon as I can."

"Just don't speed when you drive."

"I can't promise anything," my Mom said, and I could see her smile through the phone. "You know I'll be careful; I think it's you we should be worried about anyway. Don't pick any fights at Value Mart."

"Yeah, if someone grabs the Nilla Wafers when I do, they're gonna have something else coming for them," I replied.

"Sure, honey. Okay, I got to go, love you."

"Love you too, Mom."

We both hung up the phone and I started to get ready to leave, but I noticed I didn't have to. I still had everything in my pockets and my shoes on from school. I really made myself have no life when I got home.

*****

Down the Stanton Stretch past the main area and left of the police station was Value Mart: The only grocer in Stanton but never failed a citizen here. All of their items were fresh, stacked neatly, and you could start working for eight bucks an hour right when you were hired, if you were nice to the manager, which I heard wasn't that hard since he's nice to you first.

None of the people working here really had complaints about their jobs. You could work at the delicatessen (I just used that to be fancy) or the fresh fruit and vegetables market, or just as a stock boy for everything else.

My Mom had a wide variety of things I needed to get, so even if I tried to avoid taking a tour of the entire store, I'd end up going around it before I found everything. Pushing a cart along by myself, I hunted for the first thing on the list: Hotdogs.

When the hell was the last time we even had hotdogs?

I really had no idea, but maybe she was planning a cookout for after graduation or for the summer or something else like that. I didn't know. And if it was supposed to be a surprise, now it was ruined.

After grabbing a few groceries and dropping them in the cart, I noticed someone familiar checking the tomatoes.

It was Mrs. Miller.

She didn't see me, and I used that as an advantage. I wasn't really sure what she'd have to say if she saw me. I mean hell; she did call the cops on me a few days ago. Well actually… that was her husband, not her… Maybe if I just said hi.

I knew that was inappropriate though. Instead, I needed to apologize for upsetting her and dropping in unexpectedly, just like I would be now.

Taking my chances, I pushed the cart over to her and struck up a conversation.

"Hello, Mrs. Miller."

She looked up from the tomatoes and slightly gasped, but a smile appeared across her face afterward and I knew she wasn't about to throw the tomato in her left hand at me.

"Oh, hi, Jack," she replied.

"Listen, I uh, wanted to apologize for the other day—"

"No, you shouldn't," Mrs. Miller replied. "I just… really hated the thought that someone might've taken Sam's life instead of dealing with the already harsh reality that he took his own."

"I know, Mrs. Miller, and I'm sorry. I guess I was just being skeptical, like everyone else, but to a bigger extent."

"I do appreciate that though. The police officers just walked in and said it was suicide and then walked out, no questions asked. You really cared."

"Well, I tried," I replied.

Then, Mrs. Miller's face changed in a way I had never seen before. It haunted me, and even now thinking back on it, it haunts me. It was a look that only she could've done, and that was it. That's when I knew there was something more and my time wasn't wasted.

"Jack..." she started softly... so softly, I ended up leaning in to hear the rest. "You asked me... if I could put blame on someone... maybe even someone in your grade."

"Yeah, I did say that, but you don't have to—"

"Yes, Jack, actually, I do," she replied, and a few tears rolled down her face. "I didn't tell the police because I was in shock and frankly, I didn't remember it until you asked on Tuesday if I could blame someone..."

She coughed a little and I didn't urge her to say who she thought it was because then I'd feel bad.

"That night, on Monday just last week, Sam insisted for me and Jerry to go out for the night, and said he needed some time to work on something with a friend."

I almost started to cry just thinking about how Sam would've done that, knowing he was about to end his own life while thinking someone else would do it too. But, I stayed strong for Mrs. Miller as she finished the story.

She gave me a cold stare and said, "Jack, when we got back to the house, Sam's friend wasn't there... We assumed he may have never come by, but we glanced at his phone, and he had some texts from them, saying they were heading over."

"Which friend?" I asked, not sounding too demanding.

Then, she said it without knowing the true shock value behind it.

"Billy Young wasn't there."

Billy!?

"Sam said he needed to help Billy with something, and that we should just go out for the night since we never did... I wish I never did that night either," Mrs. Miller said, now starting to cry. No one else was shopping in the store, so we were pretty much alone. "Jack, don't tell anyone, please?"

"But, I have to tell the police, Mrs. Miller. Billy tricked Sam into partner suicide," I blurted, not even believing the words that were coming out of my mouth.

Why the hell would Billy do it, of all the people that could have? Billy? Billy Young? The same one I've known since sixth grade?

"No, Jack, don't, unless you can get Billy to confess to it," Mrs. Miller requested as she grabbed ahold of my shirt. "I don't know why Billy would do it, so just talk to him, okay? Maybe he didn't really do it; maybe Billy didn't know about the suicide. Maybe he never even showed up to the house once we went out? That's why I didn't mention it to the police before."

No, there was no way Billy didn't know. Why else would Sam have done it? But yet, why would Billy?

"Okay, I'll talk to him, okay?" I said with the straightest face I could.

Mrs. Miller let go of me and I stepped back to my cart, watching as she continued looking through the tomatoes and nodded at me. I knew at that point it was my time to go, and plan what I was going to do.

*****

When I finished shopping, I came home and unloaded the groceries in somewhat of a daze. At the beginning, I said Sam killing himself was too close for comfort, but now, seeing that Billy might've done it, it was way too close.

Why? Why Billy?

The sick feeling started to overcome me again and I went to my bathroom gagging.

What if Billy was going to kill me too?

When nothing came up from my stomach and my heartbeat slowed, I walked back out into my room and pulled out my cell phone, knowing what I had to do.

No, I wasn't going to tell anyone, this was now personal.

I dialed up Billy's number and waited for him to answer. When he did, I tried to sound as normal as possible, even though I wanted to flip out on him.

"Hey, Billy, look, we talked earlier about maybe hanging out sometime? How about tomorrow night?"

"Yeah, sure! Jack, are you okay?" he asked.

"Why do you ask that?" I replied, checking my tone of voice.

"Oh, nothing, just, haven't gotten any texts or calls from you in a while, so I didn't even know you still had my number. But yeah man, I really do want to hang out. Maybe we could just chill at my place?"

"Yeah, that'd be cool," I answered. "See you then."

"All right, Jack, goodnight."

I hung up my cell phone, wondering why Billy sounded so calm. It gave me the creeps, but at the same time, I thought about the possibility that he was innocent, and maybe he knew who really did it.

But no, Billy was responsible for Sam that night, and now, I am responsible for getting Billy.

CHAPTER NINE
THE KILLER
STANTON HIGH SCHOOL
FRIDAY, MAY 25TH
8 AM

Bright and early the next day, I had a brief chat with my mom over a small breakfast and then I headed to school.

Joey wasn't with his usual crowd when I pulled up, but instead, it was everyone besides him. I stepped out of my car, not really crazy about the day ahead. I just wanted the school day to end so I could end the mystery.

The crowd looked over at me and I waved subtly, to which I only got a few mean stares back. I guess Joey was the only one who liked me, even though he's probably the one who got the other guys to hate me all along.

As I walked up to the school, I felt the feeling that someone was following me, and when I turned around, I found out I was right.

"Well, I guess I wasn't being quiet enough," Alyssa said as she ran up beside me.

"What's up?" I said casually.

"Just wanted to check out a lead saying that you're bragging about me kissing you?"

"Hah, yeah, not so much bragging as I told one person and he shouted it to everyone else."

"Nick can do that sometimes," Alyssa said, but when I didn't respond and kept walking forward and looking ahead instead, she added, "What's wrong?"

"What a loaded question," I said, letting my darker side take over like it did earlier in the week. I felt like now, it was my permanent self.

"Jack, quit being so emo and just tell me."

"Really? Emo? I guess it's ninth grade all over again," I said.

Alyssa sighed and tried to fix my sorrow.

"Jack, c'mon, I didn't mean it like that."

"Alyssa," I said, and I stopped on the sidewalk heading to the school. She stopped too, and I leaned in for a spontaneous kiss that I knew she didn't see coming.

She returned it, a little surprised, but once I backed off, she looked at me deeply and asked, "Why did you do that?"

"In case I don't get to again."

With that, I walked off and she started to say something else, but she just watched me walk off to the school alone instead.

I walked in as the first bell started to ring. I didn't see Ben anywhere but I guess it didn't really matter. I preferred walking alone, especially today.

In first hour, English IV, Mrs. Reedman was ready to teach but I saw Ben on the other side of the classroom and he looked like he wanted to talk to me. I quickly said, "We can talk later," and then I headed to my seat for class to begin.

*****

Second hour, Calculus I, Mr. Harrison had a funny assignment.

"Now guys, don't start complaining, it's just a completion grade, but I just want you guys to learn, especially the ones who say everything we learn in here is useless, to realize I'm not the only one that made you do pointless things in math. Without further adieu, look at this."

It was an assignment that I didn't ever remember from elementary school. Everyone started laughing for the most part, and Mr. Harrison pestered us to actually try. I read the instructions, but it was just too weird. When had I ever learned this crap? It really wouldn't do me good now.

At the end of the hour, we were taught very briefly about the subject we were working on and then the bell rang, with Mr. Harrison's voice calling out after us that we should feel good that school's almost over. I didn't.

*****

In third hour, Sociology, nothing happened. Literally. Mr. Tinley said something about making copies at the beginning of the hour, so he left, but he never came back until the last five minutes, and then said he was sorry and didn't know it would take so long. I caught on though. I was pretty sure he did it on purpose.

*****

Fourth hour, Government, Miss Evans didn't talk to us at all today, unlike yesterday. In the meantime without any work, Emily and I got to talking about a few things.

"So, your date with Alyssa went awry, didn't it?" Emily asked with a dashing smile.

"Kind of," I answered.

"She thinks you're a strong, tough guy now," Emily added.

"Oh really?" I asked unenthused.

"Yes, she really does."

"How interesting."

Emily stared at me for a long time, trying to figure out what was wrong from how high my "surface tension" was. When she didn't know, she said, "Alyssa said something was up with you this morning. Wanna talk about it?"

"It's..." I said, trying to think of a lie. I wasn't ready to tell her everything that was going on. I couldn't bring myself to do it. I didn't even know if she knew the partner suicide theory. "It's just some stupid family stuff, that's all. My aunt thought I was crazy for using the knife on the guy."

"Really? I think it's pretty heroic, or dangerous. But I guess heroism is dangerous," Emily said sensually.

"Yeah," I said, and I started to back off.

I really didn't want to enter a love triangle, but it seemed like Emily was trying to make it that way. Maybe she just really wanted to mess with someone else and try to get rid of old feelings. I knew how that was.

"I'm... sorry Jack," Emily cut in.

"Sorry? About what?" I said, acting like I didn't know, but a part of me didn't.

"You know, coming on to you," Emily said in the most forward way ever. "I just... Not a minute goes by that I don't think about Sam and how I could've maybe saved him."

"No, quit talking like that," I said, almost tempted to spill the beans.

"It's true, Jack. I think he caught onto the fact that I wasn't very happy with him toward the end of our relationship," Emily said, shaking her head in hindsight. "It's just, he kept acting different, you know? Maybe I should've taken it as a warning sign."

I agreed with her on taking it as a warning sign, but there was nothing we could do now. I felt it was all up to me to get Sam's alleged killer, Billy Young.

But right then, I patted Emily's back lightly and promised, "It's all going to be okay."

*****

In fifth hour, Humanities, Sam's empty desk didn't seem so haunting anymore, but more of a memory of a lost kid we all cared deeply about. Miss Hannah gave us a small worksheet and I clumped into a group with Doug, Alyssa, and Emily.

Alyssa glanced at me, but we didn't talk about earlier since Doug was completely clueless on everything that was going on. I sort of envied him. As they say, ignorance is bliss.

*****

At lunch, I got through the line pretty quickly with my usual turkey sandwich and I vowed to never eat a turkey sandwich after senior year until Thanksgiving.

I saw that my always available spot by the "nerd herd" was there for me, but I decided to change it up and sit somewhere else. I just didn't know where.

Looking around, I saw Ben at the Asian table eating his lunch and laughing with his friends. He wanted to talk to me, but I didn't want to depress him with my attitude. He looked like he was having fun.

But then, Ben looked up and I made the mistake of reacting to him. He started to wave me over, and I hesitated.

No white kid had ever sat at their table or even really gone over to it. I'd feel weird if I did it.

Then I thought about it. My whole high school career, I had done things that others hadn't, inside and outside of school. I taught Raymond Todd a lesson, became Sam's best friend, and I won a fight against a mugger at Victor's Diner. So why not break the boundaries again?

So, fearlessly, I walked over to the Asian table and as I got closer, a lot of people's eyes in the lunchroom were on me, but this time, it was to see something new. Everyone was in shock, even everyone at the Asian table was shocked, besides Ben.

But I sat down just like normal to the left of Ben and said "Hi" to everyone as I sat down. The number of weird looks I got from people was amazing, but eventually, they stopped and everything returned to normal again, just like it always did in high school.

"Hi, Jack," Ben said happily.

"Hey, Ben," I replied, opening my turkey sandwich.

We let each other eat for a second before he brought up earlier.

"Did you have something to talk about? Because I did, but now I don't remember."

"Well yeah, I do have something I could talk about, but we can't say it here," I said under my breath.

"Oh, yeah, sure," Ben said, and he started to stand up.

I stood up with him and we walked over to the windows where we could look out at the parking lot. It was a view that I had forgotten about before, and it contrasted what I saw Wednesday after school.

"Look, Ben, I'm about to say something crazy, but I want you to walk away after I say it and act like we were just shooting the breeze, you got me?"

Ben's eyes widened and I knew it wasn't going to be easy for him.

"I'll try, Jack, but it seems like you have a bombshell for me."

Ignoring what he said, I informed him, "Ben, I found out who the killer probably is and I'm pursuing it tonight, and I just wanted to let you know that if I don't make it through, he will be caught and I will miss you, okay? You are a great friend and you did something good the day you suggested murder. Don't forget that."

With a final pat on the shoulder, I started to walk away from him, and his subtle response as I walked away tugged at my heartstrings.

"I'll see you at graduation, Jack."

I didn't stop and let his words affect me, but instead, I walked on and ate my lunch as I made what I knew might possibly be my final tour around the school.

*****

Before sixth hour, I called my mom asking if she could check me out before seventh hour. I just couldn't stand the idea of being around Billy until later.

"What, why honey? Everything okay?"

"Yeah, Mom, everything's fine. I just want to go home and get some quiet for a while."

"Oh, well okay, if that's what you want."

"Well also, I was wondering if I could hang out with Billy Young tonight."

My Mom tsk-ed in the phone and said, "Don't think I haven't caught on to what you're doing, Jack. You wanna skip out of school early just for the hell of it and then have fun with your friend later."

I could tell my Mom was using her joking tone, but I still defended myself.

After my defense, she said, "Okay, Jack, sure. I'll call in a little bit and let them know to check you out. And if you don't mind, I might just hang out with some people after work if you won't be home anyway."

"Yeah, that'll be fine. Thanks, Mom, I love you," I said, trying to repress the idea that it might be the last time I ever said it to her.

"I love you too, Jack, have fun."

*****

After the phone call, I walked into my sixth hour, Chemistry II, and I made my way to my seat. Everyone else settled when Miss Klein stood and had a sad announcement.

"I'm sorry, kids, but this is your last Friday here, and it's my last day here," she announced.

Only a few kids in the class actually cared and I was one of them.

When she told everyone and no one really responded, she said that today was a free day and everyone else in the room started messing around. I walked up to Miss Klein and asked what was going on.

"I have a funeral to go to next week all the way in El Paso," she started, a little torn up. "A friend from my high school died in a drunk driving accident."

"I'm sorry, Miss Klein," I said.

"No, it's okay, Jack, don't stress it. I know you've been through worse."

"No, Miss Klein, I don't think we should compare," I said, even though I was on the verge of agreeing with her.

But right when I was about to, the office called in to check me out and I felt bad about not being able to talk to Miss Klein anymore. I would've kept talking to her since I really didn't have to go anywhere, but then it'd look suspicious.

"Will you be there at graduation?" I asked before leaving.

"Eh… I'll try to Jack, maybe just for you," she said, and she flashed a smile for me.

I left feeling good for about a second but ended up still dreading tonight.

*****

I drove straight home and started to try and figure everything out. How was I even going to pull this off? What if right when I started to ask Billy about Sam, he'd flip out?

That's when I knew what I had to do to keep everything under control. I had to have the upper hand in the situation.

But, how?

124

I had never been in his house before, so I didn't know the layout. If push turned to shove, I'd have to navigate around and find somewhere to call the police. Or, I could just call the police from my cell phone.

I assigned the "P" button of my old Blackberry to be on speed dial for the police.

My heart was racing so fast I didn't know what to do with myself.

What if Billy killed me tonight? I mean, I know mostly the whole story, so I'm going to appear as a threat to him.

I started to gag again, but it didn't last long. It seems like now, the sick feeling I always seemed to feel ever since this whole thing started was starting to become a part of me. I didn't want that, but it was just the way things were.

Well, how do I let everyone else know what was going on tonight if I die? How could I prove it even when I was gone like I promised Ben?

That's when I remembered when my cousin, who I haven't seen in a very long time, and I played around with a tape recorder when we were both way younger. One of us would leave a message for the other to go do something covert, like steal a cookie or find where they were hiding. I remembered where it last was, so I headed downstairs in hopes of finding it again.

I pulled out the drawer to an old cabinet next to the front door and there it was: tape recorder and a blank tape. I popped the tape in just to see if it'd work, and then I recorded myself saying "Hi". Playing it back, the word was crystal clear with a little scratchy noise in the background that made me feel cold. I rewound the tape, put the recorder in my pocket and pressed record again, to see if it'd be muffled. I said a full sentence that I don't remember now, and when I pulled the recorder out and played it back, it was only a little muffled. Maybe my pocket wasn't the best place to put it...

So instead, I did what all the detective shows did and put it under my shirt and taped it to my chest. This time, when I recorded another sentence, it came in clearly but I still worried it wouldn't pick up Billy if he talked.

I dug around in the cabinet more and I couldn't find the little wire microphone that went along with it. Eventually, I found the original box for the recorder in the bottom of the drawer and I looked through it to find the microphone. Hooking myself up the best I could, I had the microphone wired up to my collar on the inside. So far, everything was playing in my favor, and I just hoped that's how it'd go tonight.

Just as I walked back into my room to start typing out a small letter, my phone started to ring but I checked the clock before answering it. It was 4:30, and the call was from Billy.

"Hello?" I said.

"Hey man, you weren't in seventh hour; did you get sick or something?"

"Oh, uh, no," I replied slowly as I tried to make up a quick lie. "I had a doctor's appointment that I completely forgot about."

"But, you are okay, right?"

"Yeah, just a regular checkup."

"So we're still on for tonight?"

"Yeah, we are," I said, trying to sound excited.

"Okay, well see you at seven. Do you remember where my house is?"

"Yeah, I'm pretty sure I remember."

My Mom used to pick him up when we were younger and I used to ride along. Those days seemed so innocent and so long ago.

"Are you sure you're okay, Jack? You sound … different."

I cursed myself in my head for riling him up. If I did it anymore, he was probably going to run off.

So I tried to sound as normal as possible when I said, "Yeah, Billy, I'm good. Just seemed like a long day, you know? I'm ready for some R&R with you."

My normal tone seemed to work for now.

"Ha-ha, me too man. Senior year has been such a drag."

"I know what you mean."

"Okay, well I'll let you go now. Seven at my house, okay?"

"I'll be there," I promised, but not in the way he wanted.

His line of the phone hung up and I sighed. Part of me didn't really want to go anymore, but I knew I had to.

Now that the phone call had ended, I started to write out my final note, in case everything did go bad.

It was for Chief Ramzorin, telling him where I was, what I thought, and what time I'd be there.

He was my only hope for backup.

*****

Later that night at about 6:45, I went to Shakey's and got myself a butterscotch shake and a double cheeseburger. I went through the drive-thru and then ate by myself in my car. I knew if I left the bag in, my car would reek of onions, but I didn't care. I threw it in my backseat after finishing and throwing all my trash in it and then I sucked down on the shake, in fear that I might not be on top of my game if I didn't have any dinner.

My next stop was the police station to leave the note for Chief Ramzorin. I almost hoped he wasn't there so he wouldn't have to read the note in front of me and question or scold me about it.

Luckily, when I walked into the front, the African American woman stared at me with the same sorrow she had in her eyes before.

"Jack, what can I do for you, sweetie?" she asked me nicely.

"Is Chief Ramzorin here?" I asked.

"No, he's out for dinner. I can call him up if you want."

"No, just give him this letter if you don't mind, or leave it on his desk," I requested while I handed it to her.

"Oh, sure baby," she said as she took it. Her smile came my way but I didn't return one.

"Thanks."

I walked out of the police station with too much on my mind. I couldn't calm down. The milk from the shake was just upsetting me even more, and I wondered how I could reverse everything to save Sam from Billy in the first place. But there was no way I could fly around the world and turn back time like Superman. Instead, I had to be the Punisher.

*****

Right at 7 o'clock on the dot, I pulled up to the curb of Billy Young's house that lay deep in Forest Haven. It was the only house there that looked pretty fancy and was kept up well. I wondered who did the yard work, but I decided that wasn't important as I put my car in park and turned it off.

Before walking up to the front door and having everything fall into place, I pulled up my shirt and pressed Record, and then let my shirt fall back down.

"My name is Jack Sampson, and I am about to go into the house of Billy Young, who I presume killed my best friend Sam Miller."

I kept the message short and sweet as I pulled my keys out of the ignition and stepped out of my car to head for the house.

A dog barked in the distance as I walked to his front door. The porch light gleamed above the door and I walked up in a trance of hate and rage.

No, don't do anything stupid. Just get the information and call the police.

That was my mission, but I felt like something was going to go wrong. But at that point, I didn't care about dying; I just wanted retribution for my friend.

I tried shaking it off as I pounded on his front door. Maybe that would get some of the jitters out of my system.

Soon enough, without having to ring his doorbell, I heard him run up to the door and peek out the small hole. After that, he started unlocking the several locks on the door and then opened it up.

There Billy stood, acting like everything was cool and calm. I stood there looking at him but I tried acting the same way.

"Hey, Jack, right on time. Come on in."

I did as he said and he closed the door behind me. I looked around the house to see the dimly lit living room on the right and some door to the left with a closed off hallway. I didn't know where that led, mainly because I was never able to come to his house until now. Billy was usually alone.

"Sorry about all the locks," Billy explained. "That's Donovan's way of having home security, along with that."

He pointed to the right and I saw a twelve-gauge hunting shotgun standing up against the wall.

"Careful with that; it's loaded."

I tried to make myself seem normal by making a joke.

"Yeah, I know. I remember watching the Rob the Revolver cartoons and Eddie Eagle and all that crap," I said.

"Hey! We had to watch those back at my elementary school, too," Billy said with a smile, and we both walked away from the front door. I forgot about Donovan. What would he think about all of this..?

In an awkward silence, we both looked around and had no idea what to do, until Billy asked, "Hey, do you want something to drink? I'll have to go down in the basement and get it since the refrigerator input up in the kitchen is messed up and has been since we moved here, ha-ha."

I almost said no, but then I realized that it would be an advantage to be able to corner Billy in the basement and make him talk.

"Sure, that sounds good. Just get me whatever you're getting."

"Sure thing."

Billy walked over to the mysterious door on the left and he headed down the stairs.

Okay, now he's going where I can corner him, but now what?

I had my knife on me, but I knew that wouldn't be enough, so I looked to the shotgun…

Stepping over to it, my heart started pumping harder than ever before as I picked it up by the barrel.

Kids, don't try this at home.

I checked the doorway to make sure Billy wasn't standing there watching, and as quietly as I could, I pumped the shotgun to watch one of the shells fly out. My dad had shown me how to fire one before and the safety was already off, so I knew there were still seven more shells in the chamber, which was more than enough if everything went haywire.

Then, taking a deep breath, I checked to see if the tape was still recording, and when it was, I pushed the door open to the basement with the shotgun barrel and started heading down the stairs slowly. My heart raced and my head felt heavy, but I could still walk slowly somehow.

It looked pretty bright down there, which was good. That meant there were no surprises down there for me.

As soon as I made it halfway down the stairs, Billy started walking up towards me while staring down to make sure he didn't trip and he held two cans of soda in his hands.

"Hey, Jack, I hope you don't mind diet drinks!"

"That'll be good," I replied, to get him to look up at me.

His head jerked up and he started laughing.

"Jesus, Jack! You almost scared me so badly that I'd fall down the stairs! Didn't I say not to play with that?" Billy cried out.

"I'm not playing with it, this is just a precaution," I said, stepping down toward him.

Fear struck his eyes as he started backing up into the basement again and I followed him closely. Behind him was the refrigerator he was talking about right smack dab in the middle of the back wall, followed by a door in the right corner that looked so old it was about to fall apart. A washer and dryer sat in the left corner of the back wall behind Billy, and a couch with a small TV sat to the left also. It was a man cave, where two men needed to have a serious talk.

"Jack, what are you doing?" Billy asked.

"I think you know what I'm doing, just like you did when you killed Sam."

"What?"

"Don't play dumb with me!" I shouted angrily. "Confess! I know it was you."

Then, and it made me shudder, Billy gave up the innocent look all too easy and instantly, a sinister smirk ran across his face. I was tempted to pull the trigger and end it, but I knew that would just be the beginning of a downward spiral for me.

"So, what gave it away? Did Mrs. Miller finally come to her senses and remember I was supposed to be there with Sam that night?" Billy asked as he paced backward more.

I stopped at the base of the stairwell and kept the shotgun on Billy. I held it down by my waist and tried to keep as calm as I could fighting the urge in my finger, which wanted to choke the trigger.

"So what if she did," I said. "I've been following a lead that someone killed Sam since Monday and now I've solved it."

"But I didn't kill Sam," Billy said with the same smile as before. "I made Sam kill himself."

My face was hotter than lava and I asked the question that was on everyone's mind in Stanton.

"Why?"

"That's a loaded question, Jack. And for me to answer it, we'd have to go back a little bit."

"I have all the time in the world," I answered, showing I wasn't afraid of anything.

"Okay then," Billy said, and he cracked open one of the sodas after setting the other one down on the couch. "I've been wanting to share my ingenious scheme with someone for quite a while now, although I never thought it'd be you."

"What you call ingenious, I call insanity," I countered.

"Okay, Jack, enough poetics. Everyone knows you're a smart guy. I'll tell you what happened. About nine months ago, I started to feel like I was missing something in my life, so I started to reflect. It all started in ninth grade when Sam started flirting with Emily, who I had just broken up with. Remember, when we walked in with Gary on the first day of ninth grade? She didn't care though, and she started taking an interest in him too. The next thing Sam did was he took my best friend, which was you, back before tenth grade started at the movies. I hated Sam after that, which was why I wasn't at the bowling alley on their stupid anniversary."

"Just because of a girl!?" I shouted, infuriated by the idea. "And you could've come to the movie, that was your fault."

"My fault?" Billy asked incredulously. "No, I don't think you understand. I wanted to show everyone how Sam Miller wasn't really that nice guy that everyone said he was."

"But he was!" I yelled.

"No! He wasn't. Sam Miller was just faking it to be popular in school. You don't remember the old Sam Miller, who tormented those under him. Because when people commit suicide, we try to think of everything good they did in their lifetime to show the ultimate pity, even when they're gone."

"You're wrong!" I argued, moving my finger onto and off of the trigger. *Sam was never a bad guy, or was he?*

No, Billy was just trying to get in my head and under my skin.

Billy shrugged and sighed after taking another drink. The way he was acting like everything was normal sickened me more.

"Everyone has an opinion, Jack. But anyway, after the reflection, I thought about how I should kill Sam. But, that'd be too hard to get away with, wouldn't it? I mean, murder itself usually never works out the way you need it to. So, I started talking to Sam and I thought about how he was known as a guy who never wanted to hurt anybody, so I figured if I told him he had done differently, it'd tear him up on the inside."

"You made him feel like he ruined your life, didn't you?" I seethed.

"Well, not ruined, *per se,* but I did tell him that he took my girl and he took my best friend, and so, he started to sympathize with me and tell me how sorry he was and if there was anything he could do to help. Then, I made up my plan. I told him I wanted to commit suicide, but I didn't want to go alone."

Billy took a final drink from his soda and ended up crushing the can in his hand. I flinched.

"It took me that whole nine months to convince Sam to do it with me, and the sooner to the end of the year, the better! Finally, I tore him down to the most vulnerable state I could and he said he would do it with me at his house when he got his parents to leave. I came over, with an unloaded gun from Donovan's collection, and Sam was there with a loaded pistol from his dad's collection. We sat on opposite ends of the bed and convinced each other it was the only thing we could do. I ended up counting down from three twice, and the second time, Sam did it in such a triumphant way. But I didn't applaud. I just left."

"You're lower than anyone I've ever met," I cringed. "You killed my best friend, who was the best person I had in my life, but I'm glad I took him over you."

"Oh, Jack, don't say that," Billy said, acting hurt. "It doesn't make me feel that good about myself."

"Well, you shouldn't!" I shouted. "And besides, what is Donovan going to say about all of this?"

"Funny thing about that..."

Before Billy finished, Donovan popped out from the old looking door across from me with his pistol drawn and aimed at me. I started to turn the shotgun to him, but he fired and I dropped the shotgun. The bullet sent me to the ground and my right arm felt like it was on fire and the blood was lava. I grabbed at the wound as my first reaction and I cried out in pain a few times. My legs kicked, trying to force all of the pain out, but it didn't work.

"Donovan!" I shouted. "What the hell are you doing?"

"Hah! Family first, right Billy?" Donovan asked which Billy nodded to. Donovan now acted like a high and mighty devil sent from Hell. "How else do you think the crime scene would've not shown Billy's presence? I was the first one on the scene since I'm the only detective in town. I wiped it down and made Billy never exist at the Miller's house. Billy's smart, but he still needed some help, and I was happy to."

"Why!?" I shouted, the pain still keeping me in shock. "You had nothing against Sam!"

"No, I sure didn't. But after my family threw me away and Billy's did the same for him, I vowed to always be by Billy's side no matter what," Donovan explained calmly.

I breathed heavily, trying to think about something else besides the pain. Finally, my pain on the inside started to seep to the outside.

"Okay, but if you kill me, what are you going to tell everyone else?" I asked for the sake of the tape.

"That's easy. You were deranged and desperate for an answer to Sam's suicide, so you came after my cousin with the shotgun and I was down in the basement because I forgot something for work. Easy as that," Donovan said like it was nothing.

Out of nowhere, I heard soft footsteps behind me slowly walking down the stairs and I started to look, but I didn't want to alert Billy or Donovan. They were right where they needed to be.

"So," I said, trying to sit up, "you're going to kill me now?"

"Well," Donovan started, and then he looked at Billy. "That was the plan, right?"

"Yeah, it was," Billy said back coldly.

The steps behind me were getting closer and I played along with them.

"Then what are you waiting for? Do it," I said with rage in my eyes.

"Okay, I will," Donovan said, and I saw down the barrel of his pistol, and I knew how Sam felt in his final moment. "Say hi to your dad for me in Hell."

I was just about to scream before I heard the footsteps grow louder and the person stopped right behind me with a .357 magnum up at Donovan.

"Stop!" Chief Ramzorin ordered with his revolver out.

Donovan flinched and squeezed the trigger at the same time, making the bullet hit just inches above my head. Concrete dust rained down and settled on top of my head but I didn't shake it off. Instead, I watched as Chief Ramzorin didn't hesitate at all to fire three consistent bullets into Donovan's chest, which sent him flying to the ground. My ears rang from Chief Ramzorin firing his revolver right over my head and the shots were amplified from the solid walls of the basement. Donovan's nine millimeter fell in front of Billy's feet and I saw Billy almost drop down and grab it, but Chief Ramzorin talked him out of it.

"Billy! Stop what you're doing!" Chief Ramzorin yelled. Billy slowly reached for it more and Chief Ramzorin continued, "Billy, I'm warning you, stop. You're just going to make this more of a mess than it already is, okay? Stop what you're doing and I'll guarantee you'll be safe, okay? Stop reaching for the damn gun, Billy!"

Billy looked away from the gun and saw Donovan's lifeless body on the ground. I watched as Billy started to return back to his normal state of mind as he began crying for Donovan. Chief Ramzorin lowered his pistol and walked over to the nine millimeter as Billy fell to the ground and cried over Donovan's body. I was in shock from the whole thing and I just stayed on the ground, watching as the remnants of a family were swept away in the wind.

Donovan was dead and Billy would go to jail for a long time.

It was all over.

Chapter Ten
The Graduation
The First Baptist Church
Wednesday, May 30th
6:30 pm

Let's just say, everything worked out for the best.

I was taken to the hospital shortly after everything went down but before I did, I handed Chief Ramzorin the tape recorder with all the evidence pointing to Billy Young as the man who killed Sam Miller. Or, got him to kill himself, at least.

Billy Young pled guilty right off the bat as soon as Chief Ramzorin started to question him. For that, he was only going to be sentenced twenty years and would be put up for parole in fifteen.

My Mom, Alyssa, Emily, Ben, and pretty much everyone else at my school came to visit me in the hospital that Friday night, even Joey Daniels and Gregory Allen. My Mom yelled at me for a good minute or two for doing what I had done, but afterward, she cried on my shoulder and was glad everything was okay. Emily, Ben, and Alyssa said the same thing. To them, I was the hero of our small town, Stanton.

The last three days of school flew by faster than anything, and everyone still marveled at the fact that I tackled Sam's suicide like a murder and came out victorious. All I had to show for it was a bandage over my gunshot wound on my right arm, which a lot of kids thought was cool.

Chief Ramzorin gave me a bunch of credit for finding Billy, but he was still mad at me for pursuing it. I told him I had to. I mean, Sam Miller was my best friend, and will always remain in my heart and memories.

After school on Wednesday, before I headed for graduation, I went to the cemetery that was just a little farther west of the Catholic Church in Stanton and I visited Sam's gravestone to say a few words.

"Hi, Sam," I said, not really knowing how to start. "Well, today's the big day, graduation. I… wish you could be here to share it with all of us. I bet if you were still here, you'd be able to give a speech at graduation, but… I know you're not able to."

I wiped away a few tears, still torn up about everything going on.

"I found your killer, if that's any consolation now. Honestly, Sam, I don't know why I hunted for him. Sometimes I feel like if I would've just left it alone, everything would still turn out okay. But on the other end of the spectrum, I knew it was what I had to do. I guess… I mean, my only theory of why I even went after it, was… my Dad was taken away from me, and I wasn't able to do anything about it. But when you killed yourself, and Ben said it was murder and not suicide, well, I knew there was something I could do; maybe not to get you back, but to keep your memory strong in the eyes of others. I love you, Sam. I'm going to miss you a lot, and for the rest of my life. But you'll always be with me, no matter what, and I'll remember all the good times we had together when I'm alone and down on my luck, or just struggling in general. Because… that's what friends are for."

I left the graveyard crying my eyes out, promising myself again that it'd be my last time to cry. It didn't seem right to stay there and cry it out, because I had other things to do, and I knew that by now if Sam was looking down on me, he was probably annoyed at how much I cried and mourned his death. That made me smile and start to calm down and not cry as much as I stepped into my car and drove home. It seemed like the longest drive I had ever taken, but it was worth it to see Sam once more.

My Mom greeted me at the door and I was surprised. She said she'd make it out to the graduation, but she didn't mention seeing me before.

"How could I miss this, Jack?" she asked after I expressed how surprised I was.

"I knew you wouldn't miss it, but I thought you'd be there later," I said, hugging her.

Eventually, we parted and she told me to go put on my cap and gown. I ran up to my room and she said she was going to hunt for a camera. Looking through my closet, I found the gown pretty quickly and threw it on over my clothes I already had on. I looked at myself in the mirror and felt really old. This was the moment I was supposed to be waiting for and anticipating all year, but I just started to get the butterflies once I saw myself in the mirror.

When I walked back down to my Mom, she held the small Nikon digital camera in her right hand and covered her mouth in amazement with her left.

"Oh my God, Jack…"

"I know. I felt old looking in the mirror," I said as I tried to walk down the stairs without tripping.

She smiled with tears already filling in her eyes and she steadied the camera. The camera flashed before I was even ready but she acted like she'd get a better picture later.

"Your Dad would be so proud of you," my Mom said sweetly.

"Yeah," I said softly, thinking back on my dad.

*****

My Mom drove me to The First Baptist Church in whatever city it was and we pulled up in the parking lot to see all of my other classmates walking around in their caps and gowns. She gave me another hug as we stretched over the center console and she said I should go ahead and join them.

I stepped out of my Mom's Honda Civic and made my way over to Alyssa, Ben, Emily, Harold, Mark, and Nick.

"Hey, Jack!" they all greeted me.

"Hi, guys," I said. "Excited?"

"Yeah!" most of them said.

Nick singled himself out by saying, "I'm nervous about MIT."

"You got in!?" I asked. "Why didn't you ever talk about that?"

"It's not that big of a deal," Nick said.

"Yeah, but a glitch in Grave Robber is?" I joked, and I punched him in the arm in a kidding way but my right arm ached afterward. I clutched at the wound and everyone moved with me.

"Are you okay, Jack?" Emily asked.

"Yeah, I'm good guys, don't worry," I said. "If it put away Sam's killer, it was worth it."

Ben cut in to share his feelings.

"I can't believe it was Billy though... Who would've thought?"

"I know," Alyssa agreed. "I thought he was a nice guy."

"So did I, until he told his cousin to kill me," I said.

Everyone cringed at the thought and then Harold said, "I heard Billy's parents are driving in to see him."

"Really?" Emily asked. "But, aren't they..."

"I guess they're a little cleaner than they used to be," Harold answered.

"That's good," Alyssa commented.

"Yeah, it is," I said.

The sun was setting off in the west and I could see the orange and purple clouds over the top of the church. Being in the forest town of Stanton, I never really got to see any sunsets, and it really took my breath away.

"All students begin to find your walking buddy," Principal Leonard announced over a bullhorn out in the parking lot.

"Okay, well I guess this is it," Emily said with obvious excitement.

"Yeah, see you guys on the other side," I replied.

Our group started to disperse in different directions and just as I was about to find Max Silberstein, Alyssa grabbed me and said, "Hey."

I turned around and she pulled me in for a random kiss that I accepted graciously. We held it there for a few seconds and then parted.

"What was that for, good luck?" I asked.

"I'm not Princess Leia," Alyssa started, "I just wanted to do that. You know, in case I didn't get to again."

And just like that, she strolled off to find her buddy and I knew she was mocking me from the other day, but I guess it was good to make light of the situation.

*****

When graduation started at seven, I walked out with Max Silberstein to the seats as the adults cheered for the students walking out. The whole experience felt surreal, and I knew it was finally over. High school was done. Now I was going to graduate and... well, I wasn't really sure yet what else I'd do. Chief Ramzorin made a joke about hiring me as a detective, but maybe it wasn't really a joke.

But I thought I wouldn't like that line of work. It would always remind me of Sam, and how I fought through the tears and the pain just to find who killed him.

I glanced out in the crowd to check and see if I saw anyone. First, I saw my Mom with Miss Klein sitting next to her. I waved at both of them and Miss Klein waved back while my Mom cheered for me. Next, I saw Chief Ramzorin giving me a thumbs up which I returned. Then, I looked over to the side where only a few people sat and I saw two people that I didn't expect to see.

Mr. and Mrs. Miller sat over on the side by themselves, but they both waved at me. I waved calmly at them and continued walking to my seat.

First was the National Anthem followed by the Pledge, which seemed to take longer than usual today. But, I was proud to be at the graduation and not over in some war-torn country like my Father had been.

I missed him, and I missed Sam, but I knew both of them were watching down on me and they were proud of what I had done.

Finally, Principal Leonard began to talk and my fingers itched to get my diploma.

"Ahem. I'd like to go ahead and thank everyone for coming out here today to this beautiful church, which was kind enough to let us have our ceremony here tonight," Principal Leonard said in his dark black robes and everyone clapped for about twenty seconds, and then he continued talking when it died out. "Now, Class of 2012, congratulations. This year, we overcame some unexpected challenges, but you all took it on like it was nothing. Furthermore, I'd like to give one of our students from Stanton High a little bit of recognition for something he did just because of the power of friendship, and how when we lose friends, we can still be driven in our hearts to do something in their memory."

Just as Principal Leonard started to say who it was he wanted to thank (although I think it's pretty obvious who he's going to say), I looked over at the back of Alyssa's head and she turned around to look back at me, and we made eye contact for the longest time. My heartbeat was calm as my stomach felt butterflies more than ever. I knew what needed to be said and done with her after graduation.

"Ladies and gentlemen, I'd like to give great thanks and lots of admiration to a man who stood up to a mystery most of us didn't know existed, and he solved it with the help of a few of his friends. Please, give a big round of applause to someone who I didn't know very well until two weeks ago and now I'm very glad I do know him, Mr. Jack Sampson."

As the clapping began, Principal Leonard signaled me to stand up and I did. The clapping and cheering grew louder and louder and I felt I was about to blush. But then, I didn't really know why I was going to blush. I wasn't ashamed of what I had done; I was actually quite the opposite. I was proud of myself, and everyone else around me was too.

The clapping escalated more and more and I stood as a few more people around me stood up just to give me a standing ovation.

But, I guess that's what happens when you solve the murder of a person who never should have been killed in the first place.

ABOUT THE AUTHOR

Henry Cline was born in 1994 in Oklahoma City, Oklahoma. He has been writing since he was seven and started writing novels at the age of eleven. His other passions include playing the electric guitar, cooking, and baking. His first album, 'Resilience', was released in September of 2016.